The Tormenting of Lafayette Jackson

The Tormenting of Lafayette Jackson

Andrew Rosenheim

David R. Godine · Publisher
BOSTON

First edition published in 1988 by
DAVID R. GODINE, PUBLISHER, INC.
Horticultural Hall
300 Massachusetts Avenue
Boston, Massachusetts 02115

Library of Congress Cataloging in Publication Data
Rosenheim, Andrew.
The tormenting of Lafayette Jackson.
I. Title.
PS3568.O818T67 1988   813'.54   87-45456
ISBN 0-87923-704-X

FIRST EDITION
Printed in the United States of America

for Claire

Only the insane take themselves quite seriously.
Lord David Cecil, MAX

The Tormenting of Lafayette Jackson

One

When I landed at Heathrow, the terminal was being remodeled. There is an unprogressive appearance to all English construction; it is usually impossible to tell whether the workmen smoking cigarettes and drinking tea are erecting a building or pulling it down. In New York, any similar confusion is hailed as a sure sign of Decline, denounced in some dreary article by a local Spengler. At Heathrow, it seemed perfectly normal.

I took the bus to Reading. The fields had grown green in my month's absence and I smoked cigarettes to stay awake and enjoy them. On the connecting train from Reading, I bought a cup of coffee and stood staring out the window at the familiar countryside. There is a beautiful stretch of the Thames on the far side of the town and I noticed the water was high, pushing up over the bank on the far side. By the time the Oxford spires came into view—not intrusively, but as a telling, aesthetic backdrop to the city's trashy urban renewal—I felt oddly and thoroughly at home.

My luggage made the short walk to the college from the station impossible, so I splurged on a taxi. It was just seven-thirty when the cab turned off St. Aldates, and as I paid the fare I saw no one but Buggins, the head porter's cat, slinking into the Lodge. Very early morning is the best time to visit Oxford, for the landscape is unpeopled then, and the city is such a Western monument it is a rare thing to see it unencumbered, without cameras, without guidebooks, without tourists.

My mail was sparse: a form letter from the Dean, a college library overdue notice. Nothing, naturally enough, from the States since I had just come from there. I entered the old quad and saw that the flower boxes were filled, perched perilously on window ledges around the quad. They were the ephemeral products of great pains; when I thought of what they cost to put in, and how little time they lasted, I realized I'd been too long in New York. In Chapel Quad the tulips were beginning to bloom; bursts of scarlet, pink and yellow ranged across the north wall near a dull, dry, permanently deadened patch of ground by the Fellows Garden where the rugby team had vomited en masse the year before.

When I walked into North Quad there was no one about. My steps echoed from the paving stones; they had been newly laid in autumn but had already assumed the dull yellow color of the college's stone. A light shone in the Dean's rooms; he was an early riser said to finish the *Times* crossword each day before breakfast. In Eden Hall, where my room was, the noise of a shower rang like a small chain rattling in the air. On the stairs I found Emily, my scout. We eyed each other warily.

"It's you," she said flatly, and there seemed no reason to confirm this with a reply. On Emily's head sat the usual wig of gold and crimson curls; her face was a mixture of Scottish freckles and Woolworth's lipstick. I had not expected a scout out of *Brideshead*, but Emily had still been a surprise.

"You've started early," I said, not really meaning her work. Rum is not effectively masked by Indian tea, however strong.

"It's hard work," she said automatically, and added,

"You've been in the States." She rolled an obvious eye at my duty-free shopping bag.

I sighed and put down the plastic bag, extracting a liter bottle of Beefeater gin. I handed it to her and she nodded approvingly. "A generous act," she said insincerely, "most generous indeed."

"Have a nice day," I said with sardonic resignation and moved past Emily up the stairs. I was left with a single bottle of bourbon but supposed my gift of gin would at least have the prophylactic effect of preserving the Jack Daniel's for a week or so. It would also keep Emily from reporting me to the Dean should I go to London for a couple of days during the term. Or smuggle a girl into my room, no longer an impossibility since the termination of my engagement.

"Finals this term then?" she called after me, perhaps to modify the cynicism of our transaction. I nodded my head and kept walking. "Work hard," she said with a loud cackle of laughter, for she knew my ways. "Just like Michael Shambling."

Just like Michael Shambling indeed, I thought as I came to my room. He was an English undergraduate in my year; we had shared a tutorial one term in Political Institutions, and Shambling had complained to the tutor that I wasn't keeping up with the required reading. In turn, I'd threatened to pour lager all over his back issues of *New Society*, and our relations thereafter soured.

My room showed evidence of Emily's cleaning; it was very neat, almost sterile. Eden Hall was a new dormitory built along the lines of a Holiday Inn. I had mixed feelings about this modernity, depending on the season. In winter, showers and central heating were rare pleasures, much envied by my friends; in spring, the tables turned and I was jealous of their two-room suites and Tudor beams. That morning, I poured myself two fingers of sherry and got into bed with an old copy of the *Spectator*. I read Auberon Waugh. I tried to read an editorial. I fell asleep, my mind a virtual *tabula rasa* for the term that lay ahead.

I woke up a little after teatime, which in my life then was cocktail hour. I showered and got dressed, then left my room to go to see McCandles.

He lived across St. Aldates in the grandeur of Christ Church. My college was smaller, poorer, and celebrated chiefly in an age-old joke as Christ Church's coal bin. Yet I would not have traded places with McCandles, for there was a privacy to my college I enjoyed; the tutors, I should add, were also less demanding. I walked through Tom Quad, past Mercury where no one I knew had ever been dunked. Descending the steps by the dining hall I reached the mud of Meadow Quad and trod carefully to the archway and McCandles' rooms. Both outer and inner doors were open and I went in cautiously, knocking first. McCandles was my closest friend at Oxford, or anywhere for that matter, but he was fastidious in matters of social protocol. This showed in his clothes, which were expensive and well-made, even in casual wear; it was reflected, too, in a certain reserve he brought to all relationships.

I found him, wrapped in a silk dressing gown, standing on a coffee table facing the window and Christ Church Meadows. McCandles was short enough to make his posture ridiculous, but the sharp cut to his jaw and sheer sternness of his gaze kept my laughter in check. The same mix of sublime and ridiculous could be found in the appearance of his rooms. They were luxurious, with high ceilings and elaborate wainscotting, and, in contrast to the rust-orange and institutional green of my own smaller and more modern quarters, they were painted in an ornate blend of cream and gray. But they were also penuriously cold. McCandles claimed he constantly suffered from chillblains and went to bed each night with a hot water bottle.

"I'm sorry to interrupt you," I said in a loud voice, "but the Dean would like to know the reasons for your vigilant inspection of the Meadows."

"Hello James," said McCandles in a parody of British coolness. He did not turn round. "There were nuns in the grounds just a little while ago; several nuns. I want to ask them in for tea. Then perhaps a little entertainment." He gestured obscenely with the belt of his robe.

"You'd charge them for the tea?"

"Of course." McCandles got down from the table and sat across from me in an ancient padded leather chair. "You remember Cantucci?" He spoke in the clipped Southern interrogative I always find surprising. I was brought up to think that any descent south of the Mason–Dixon line signified an aural decline into mush-filled drawls.

"I tried to forget him," I said.

"Apparently he founded quite an enterprise in Magdalen. His rooms looked over the deer park and he would lure the tourists in for tea. Charge them a pound a head for brown water and stale scones."

"Have tea with a real live Oxford Undergraduate?"

"Exactly. With the Americans, he'd play the poor country boy, set down in the alien world of tutorials and quinine water. He's from Iowa, you know. With the Germans and Japs, he'd be extremely British. 'So very glad to see you.'"

"And?"

"And?" McCandles looked abstracted, fingering his robe. He had bought it in Jermyn Street with an astonishingly large part of the five hundred dollars sent by his parents for the purchase of a formal dinner jacket. McCandles liked to discuss what he should tell them he did with the money. The remainder had gone to a gambling club we'd joined in London the year before.

"Oh," he said, returning to the conversation, "the upshot was that Cantucci cleared more than three hundred pounds but then one afternoon three skinheads came to tea and wiped him out. They took off his trousers, carved a crude swastika on his ass with a penknife, then robbed him of virtually everything he owned. They even took his Magdalen tie."

"How do you know all this?"

"Sally Archimedes told me. One night she got drunk and in a fit of compassion slept with Cantucci. Halfway through, he started crying and told her the whole story."

Sally was a Rhodes Scholar of fierce ambition and voluminous thighs. She wanted badly to be a famous journalist and worked during vacations as a "stringer" for *Newsweek*.

"And then she runs off and tells you."

"It took half a bottle of Scotch to get the whole story. I was scared I'd have to sleep with her to hear it all."

I laughed. "So how have you been?"

"So-so," he said with a shrug. "I've worked the last two weeks, but only because there wasn't anything else to do. Audrey was here for a week and got so bored she went back to London. No one else has been around and I swore I wouldn't go travelling. How about a drink?"

Without waiting for an answer, he made us each a stiff gin and lime, "No ice, I'm afraid," he said. "The bugger's fridge is out." He referred to Prince Rupert von Eckstein, a German aristocrat (any nobility, however dubious, was recognized by Christ Church). Eckstein lived across the hall and had the habit of asking McCandles to come in and talk when he was taking a bath. There was always a pretext: once Eckstein had left his soap in his room, another time his shampoo, and on yet another occasion he demanded the *Times* be brought in so he could read the theater listings that sit in miniaturized type on the bottom of the arts page. The homoerotic implications of the ritual irritated McCandles, a confirmed heterosexual despite a certain dandyism, and a self-proclaimed prude.

"So, how was the States?," he asked me.

"Not so good. My grandfather died."

"I'm sorry," McCandles said and paused, then added hopefully, "Of unnatural causes?"

"For Christ's sake, Wilmarth, he was ninety-three years old. What do you expect at that age—suicide?"

"Did he leave you any money?"

"Actually, it looks like he did. At least my father says he did."

"How much?"

"I've no idea," I said primly. "I'm sure it's not very much. A couple of grand maybe."

"Lucky you!"

"On the whole I'd rather have my grandfather."

McCandles looked at me with pitying incomprehension, then merely shrugged and diplomatically changed the subject. "Did you have any fun at all?"

"Not much." I paused. "I did play golf with my brother. That was fun."

"What did you shoot?"

"85 one day, 89 the other."

"Not bad." Like me, McCandles recognized that no matter how terrible the people who play it, golf itself is essentially sound. "You went to New York?"

"I flew back from there."

"And?"

I took a swallow of my drink. "She wouldn't change her mind."

"Just like she said in the letter?"

"Worse. She's in love with one of her teachers."

"You must be joking."

"I know, it's hard to believe."

"I suppose it's one of the benefits of a captive relationship. I mean really," he said with irritation, "next to being a psychotherapist I should think teachers have more sway over people than anyone else. Whoever this fellow is he must be very irresponsible."

"I said that to Carol."

"And what did she say?"

"She said she expected as much from me. Essentially her view is that I'm socially retarded and conceptually premature."

"Conceptually what?"

"This teacher's a cognitive psychologist. Frankly, he sounds like he should be working in one of those Soviet asylums where they send political prisoners. He's persuaded Carol that I'm in something called the pre-formative stage. Presumably, she's already forming."

"Forming what?"

"I don't know. Attachments to older men. She'll still be my friend she said. Apparently you can be nice to people left in the dark ages of the pre-formative stage."

McCandles snorted. "What did you say to that?"

"I told her I didn't need any more friends. She regressed to the pre-formative stage and got mad. I haven't talked to her since."

"So that's that."

"Yes," I said with finality, sensing that McCandles was more bothered than he showed. He was getting married in the summertime—his fiancée had come over to London to be near him—and he had used the prospect of my proposed marriage to allay his doubts about his own. Now this comforter was out of feathers.

"What do your parents think?"

"They are greatly disappointed," I said dryly. "In some ways they like Carol more than they like me."

"So what are you going to do?" he asked, a little anxiously.

"What can I do? I'll just try to forget the whole thing. I've got Finals at the end of term to keep me occupied."

McCandles nodded skeptically. "Sometimes I can't make you out at all. Something trivial goes wrong and you act neurotic for a week. Then something important happens and you just shrug it off. It's as if your Jewish side was at perpetual odds with your Yankee blood—'oy vay' competing with a stiff upper lip."

I said nothing in reply, feeling I could do without such probings. "Anyway," McCandles said, "tell me about New York. Did you have a good time there?"

"God, what an awful place. 'Where the inhabitants mistake neurosis for energy'," I quoted. "Why does it have to be the one place where I'll have to live?"

"There are other cities to work in," McCandles said mildly.

"Not in journalism, at least not for magazines. Well, at least not places where *I* can get a job."

"You sound fairly provincial."

"You're right, but I blame New York for that. Considering how cosmopolitan it's supposed to be, New York has the curious ability of making you forget that there are other places to live. Sane places, even, with sane people."

"How are things in Michigan?"

"You mean at home? The same as ever. My sister went back to her shrink."

"Why? Is she *really* crazy now?"

"Not at all. She's just depressed."

McCandles looked disappointed. "Honestly, I'm tired of people saying they're depressed. I'm only interested in real crazies. Who cares about depression? I'm depressed ninety percent of the time; you don't see *me* entering a mental ward."

There seemed something askew with McCandles' assessment, but I didn't say so. He tended to be impatient with weakness. Now he shook his head and fixed himself another drink. He pointed out the window with his free hand. "I can't wait for the time to change. I hate it when spring's coming and it still gets dark this early."

"So do I." It always reminded me of boarding school in Massachusetts, of walking back from the squash courts in the dark with nothing to look forward to except a bad dinner and three hours in the library. Everybody else there seemed to like winter—the hockey games on Saturday night, the hot cider served by the headmaster's wife, the skiing weekends in Vermont. I hated it all.

McCandles kept staring out the window. "At home we used to call it the dark season," he said gloomily. "Once the time changed in spring my father would announce that the 'dark season' was over. Yet he always claimed it was after the time changed that the suicide rate picked up dramatically."

"Among his patients?"

"By the dozens," McCandles said more cheerfully.

There was a noise at the door and Newcastle came in. He nodded at us both, smiling weakly. He was an English acquaintance of McCandles with a fascination for things American and the common aptitude among foreigners for jumping to quick conclusions about the States. He and McCandles shared an adviser whom they both despised; when I saw Newcastle it was always with McCandles, and the two of them would invariably begin talking about this adviser, a man named Hubert, in low tones of deep derision. This was his only tie with McCandles; I had never heard them talk about anything else. Lacking even this one topic, I found conversation with Newcastle entirely infertile. I suppose I mildly disliked him; probably he reciprocated this feeling.

I knew that Newcastle was supposed to be poor, not a common condition in Christ Church, and that even though he'd taken a First Class Honours degree in the History Schools and been a graduate student for over eighteen months, he felt himself an outsider in college. He was a socialist, moreover, in a college that still had trouble swallowing Robert Peel, and although to us Americans these vestiges of class warfare were oddities to treasure (they formed a rare link between Oxford as pictured on the other side of the Atlantic and the place as we found it), they were considerably less amusing to those English students who suffered from them.

Ironically, considering his class antipathies, Newcastle's mother was a lawyer—a solicitor in London and highly successful. His father had left them both while Newcastle was still in diapers. Faced with the choice between child and career, his mother had shipped Newcastle off at an early age to her own parents in the north. They were humble people—Newcastle's grandfather worked as a clerk for a consortium of dairy cattle middlemen—so Newcastle grew up in the north country with the repressed personal habits of the lower middle class. He ate tea instead of dinner in the evening, and had beans on toast thrice weekly as a matter of course. His natural intelligence, deposited no doubt by the superior genes of his formidable mother, saw Newcastle to grammar school on a scholarship, then through to Oxford with the benefit of three A's in the A-level exams.

This intelligence may also have caused him to reject the implicit political philosophy of his childhood milieu (Grandpa was an unabashed Tory) and to adopt a personal politics of extreme, class-conscious, left-wing socialism. It was not evident in his clothes or in his manner, but in argument he could be quick to lash out at any proposition to the right of Trotsky, and "fascist" was his standard term of disapproval. That deep down he knew that he was neither of the working class he professed to admire, nor really of the *petit bourgeoisie* which stamped his daily life as a boy, made his hatred of the professional classes—and therefore of his mother—that much stronger.

Newcastle's personal history had emerged in a series of conversations with McCandles during the previous year; but this kind of social analysis was mine and had never interested McCandles, for whom British class refinements in the strata between baronetcy and dukedom alone were worthy of notice.

"So what do you think about the elections?" Newcastle asked me now, like a graduate student tackling his teacher after class. Oddly, it was America's wealth and power—its unbridled consumerism—that seemed most to interest him. As if flashy cars and expensive tailoring were somehow democratized by their stepping westward. These things, and the minutiae of the Washington political scene, held a glamor for Newcastle; they bored me stiff. But ever since McCandles had told Newcastle that I had worked briefly in journalism in New York, I was clearly expected to "keep up." I usually had the nagging feeling that I was letting Newcastle down.

"What elections? There're no elections now."

"The primaries, of course."

I didn't have anything to say. Fresh from lamenting winter's persistence with McCandles, I found it impossible to project forward to the following fall. Besides, that was a different world altogether; I didn't even read the *International Herald Tribune* anymore. For all that I might share in mocking Oxford with McCandles—poking fun at its incredible insularity, the dry effeminacy of the dons, the prolonged adolescence of its undergraduates—I was, in fact, very happy there. Happy in the paradoxically plaintive fashion of all young men. Happy, too, because the strongest negative emotion I felt at Oxford was boredom.

Now McCandles, sensing my unwillingness to talk politics with his friend, changed the subject. "Have you seen Hubert?" he asked Newcastle. He also handed him a drink, which Newcastle sipped timidly. It was my guess he was more at ease with beer than spirits, and that even with a pint in his hand he was not relaxed. He suggested nothing so much as a schoolboy cramming for the Oxford Entrance Exams, furtively sneaking a shandy on a half-hour break from his books.

"I hate that man," Newcastle announced, sweeping his hair out of his eyes. Even for that late day and age Newcastle's hair was a little long, and it never struck me as particularly clean.

"What's Hubert done now?" I asked.

"He's trying to do me in, is what. I have to receive approval for my thesis topic this term, and he's threatening to revoke his support."

On the surface, it was hard to understand why Newcastle had such difficulties with his adviser; they shared an equally intense interest in America. In fact, Hubert was really the doyen of American historical studies at the university. He punctuated his Oxford life of tutorial supervision and doctoral students with annual trips to the States during the Long Vac each summer. Perhaps it was a measure of his dedication to the New World that he seemed to find something unpleasant, almost spurious in any other Britons who studied American history. Among his students, he far preferred the genuine American article, claiming a Saltonstall, a Lehman, and a McCormick among the ranks of Americans who had passed, or suffered, through his tutelage.

Recounting his conversation with the man, Newcastle now grew excited. When this happened, his hands would move in a flurry of rapid, chopping movements, something like a chef dicing vegetables. "He said there was little evidence to indicate that I should be moved up. He went on like that—the pompous fascist shit—and said he thought I might be lacking the necessary maturity required for a doctorate."

McCandles laughed, but Newcastle looked so pained that I forewent the pleasure of joining in. There was an almost disturbing intensity about Newcastle that was belied at first by the shyness and conventional rattiness of his appearance.

"What does he want you to do?" asked McCandles, without excessive concern, for he planned to attend American law school the following autumn, and his admission would not be affected by the condition of his own thesis.

"I don't know. He said he expected marked improvement in my work this term or I could not expect any support from him. To be honest, I think he probably wants to wash his hands of me. He got rid of Christopher Pollard last spring, you know, but Pollard just switched over to political philosophy. He's all right—he'll get his D.Phil."

"Why don't you switch?" I suggested.

McCandles answered for him. "He'd have to switch thesis topics."

"Well, what's wrong with that?"

"No," said Newcastle curtly. "I don't want to switch topics. And besides, I have a good topic as it is."

"What is your topic?" I asked with some embarrassment, thinking that if I were to be involved in the conversation I had better acquaint myself with its suppositions.

"The antebellum abolitionists in the Carolinas," he said rapidly, with the rigorous certainty of a biochemist reciting the compounds that came under his purview.

"Interesting," I said as politely as possible.

McCandles looked at me with a mixture of humor and scorn. "There weren't any," he said.

"What?"

"Abolitionists in the Carolinas," he barked. "There weren't any."

Newcastle interjected, "I wouldn't go as far as that. I'm certain there had to have been some. It's just . . . " he said hesitantly, almost sheepishly, "I'm having a little difficulty finding them."

"Is that what's bothering Hubert?" I asked.

"Heavens no," said Newcastle. "He doesn't care about anything that happened in your country before 1943."

"Why 1943?"

"That's when he was seconded to the embassy in Washington."

I found this all confusing and excused myself to use McCandles' lavatory. I ran into Eckstein in the hall and exchanged prolonged and faintly bogus pleasantries. When I returned to the room, Newcastle had his coat on and was about to go.

"So you see," he was saying, "she's my only real chance. If she'll take me on everything will work out very well. If she won't, I'm stuck with Hubert and you know what that means."

"Maybe you can show him a new maturity," said McCandles with a grin.

"Perhaps," said Newcastle without smiling back. "Anyway, I must run. Goodbye and thank you for the drink. Goodbye James."

I said goodbye and Newcastle shut the door behind him. He had very formal manners; even the etiquette-conscious McCandles thought them excessive.

"What was all that about?" I asked as I resumed my seat.

"He's in trouble. Hubert doesn't like Newcastle very much and Newcastle makes things worse by provoking Hubert."

"How's he do that?"

"Hubert loves to boast about his Second World War days at the embassy. You'll be sitting in a seminar listening to some Canadian talk about the Underground Railway in Saskatchewan when Hubert will suddenly interrupt to explain what race relations were like in Georgetown during the war. I don't know which is more boring—Saskatchewan Unitarians or the war as seen from the 'colonies.' But Newcastle pretends to be fascinated, almost sycophantically so, until he suddenly starts asking Hubert embarrassing questions. Once Hubert told us about a drive he took with Harold Ickes along the Potomac the day news came of the D-Day invasion. Newcastle spent the next ten days researching the matter and discovered that Harold Ickes was in Mexico when the invasion took place. Naturally, Newcastle took the first public occasion to ask Hubert about the discrepancy."

"And what did Hubert say?"

"What could he say? He blushed and hemmed and hawed and finally said that perhaps he'd got the date wrong."

"No wonder he doesn't like Newcastle. But if Hubert won't let him transfer to the D. Phil., what's Newcastle going to do?"

"I have no idea. Go on the dole, I suppose, like everybody else seems to do in this country. It's remarkable, when you consider how hard it is for the Brits to get into Oxford, how little good it does them. Newcastle had one of the best Firsts in his year and he couldn't have got a job shining shoes in Paddington Station."

"Can't he try to patch things up with Hubert?"

"It's too late for that. I should think the damage was irreparable. His one hope now is in going to see this woman."

"Who's that?"

"Her name is Lafayette Jackson. She's the historian who's here to deliver the Wise lectures."

"I think I've heard of her."

"She writes for the *TLS*. Long, boring articles about ante-bellum politics in the South."

"My God."

"Exactly. She also wrote a book about an island in the Mississippi that disappeared in an earthquake in 1810 or something."

"That sounds a little like Newcastle's abolitionists."

"I know, but she actually found some evidence, letters

from a plantation owner on the island. Apparently, there was an enormous slave colony on this island which nobody's ever known about until Jackson found these letters."

"What a find."

"I'll say. I mean, there are always letters being found in attics down South; even my father has some in the garage that were written by one of my ancestors who owned a plantation in South Carolina. But usually the letters aren't very interesting; they're all about furniture they've ordered from France. Jackson's letters were full of detail about slave life; how many babies the housegirls had, what the field hands ate for Christmas. That sort of thing. They're simply a goldmine of information. This book of hers is the only one she's written but it made her famous."

"What's the book called?"

"I don't know; *Love In a Hot Climate*, or something like that. I never read it. But it's certainly Newcastle's field. Hubert doesn't know much about slavery, or abolitionists for that matter, so he told Newcastle to go see this woman and ask if she'll be his adviser. I think Hubert just wants to get rid of him."

"Maybe Jackson will take Newcastle on."

"I wouldn't count on it. She's only here for a term, and I bet the last thing she needs is a thesis to direct from four thousand miles away."

"Especially if it's Newcastle's."

McCandles nodded. "There *is* something a little touched about the fellow."

Two

I was more depressed about the termination of my engagement than I had let on to McCandles. The prospect of finishing at Oxford and returning to America no longer seemed, well, *reasonable*. There was no wife-to-be in New York anymore, and I was beginning to wonder if there was any point in going back there. I didn't even like the place; if I had not won one of three scholarships annually awarded for study abroad by my home state of Michigan, I would have been still sitting at a desk somewhere in Manhattan, writing captions and wondering when I would get made an associate editor. Increasingly I was feeling that I had made a lucky escape. Surely there were jobs to be had elsewhere, though what and where I didn't know.

Feeling dislocated and uncertain about my future, I tried settling down to my work. I didn't see McCandles for over a week; I was busy with the delicate art of appeasing my tutors. I had almost failed a mock-exam in Russell and Wittgenstein and since my finals loomed at the end of term, I thought I'd better discuss my poor performance with my tutor in philosophy, Mr. Hopkins. Although I had a full term in which to revise, this leeway wasn't especially comforting, since so little of what I'd read—or was supposed to have read—had stuck the first time around.

Mr. Hopkins was a bachelor don, increasingly rare in modern-day Oxford, with a sharp tongue and an erratic facial tic that scared the first-year students. I rather liked him, but he seemed to have ambivalent feelings about me; he had long since given up on my chances for First Class Honours and seemed disinclined to provide much in the way of further instruction. That week, I tackled him twice in an effort to get him to see me, but both times—once in Hall after dinner, once in the Porter's Lodge when he went to fetch his mail—he successfully dodged me, bustling by with a great sweep of his black M.A. gown and a convoluted series of tics. Finally, I wrote him with obsequious formality, requesting an appointment to talk about my mock-exam. The next morning I found a card from him in my box which read in its entirety:

> "Whereof we cannot speak,
> thereof we must remain silent. H."

This was enough to dissuade me from further importuning. My work lapsed into novel-reading; one evening, when McCandles stopped by my room, he found me finishing Waugh's war trilogy.

"How was it?" he asked, accepting a whiskey from the bottom of my duty-free bottle.

"Excellent. I like it even better than the early novels."

"Not a view shared by the critics."

"Screw the critics. They just don't like his Catholicism. Look at Edmund Wilson; he's entirely put off by the conversion in *Brideshead*."

"Aren't you?"

"Not at all. I find it very plausible."

"So do I," said McCandles sadly. I laughed but felt on dangerous ground. As the product of a hybrid marriage I hold no belief in any religion but have an intrinsic, probably unfounded respect for them all. The deep South, McCandles assured me, took matters more seriously; it was so Protestant, he said jocularly, that it was better to marry an amputated Jew than any kind of Catholic. This made his own latent love of Catholicism, which emerged only in his bleakest moments, that much more dangerously alluring.

"Have another drink," I said now, pouring him more bourbon.

"Put some water in it, please."

"Try it first." I handed him the glass and he took a cautious sip.

"It's got water in it already," he said in surprise.

"Emily."

"Your scout?"

I nodded. "She takes a belt each day and replaces it with water. Wait two weeks and you'll be asking me to put more bourbon in the glass."

"Can't you lock up your liquor?"

"I do," I said, pointing to a desk drawer. "But she's got the key."

"Those rich Yanks," he said in an excellent imitation, " 'What do they know about spirits? He'll never notice a wee drop.' "

"So," I said, sitting down, "has anything been happening?"

"The usual. Sally Archimedes slept with the cultural attaché at the London Embassy."

"How do you know?"

"She told me, how else? She's decided that all men ever tell each other is who they've been fucking. So every time I see her now she recites her latest conquest. She was very proud of this one, though he's obviously not much of a cultural attaché."

"Why? Because he slept with Sally?"

"Partly. But also because I met him at a reception for American students. When I asked him what he thought about repatriating the Elgin Marbles he didn't know what they were. He must be a CIA agent; they say the cultural attaché always is. But I tell you, American intelligence is in trouble if this fellow's anything to go by. It's a far cry from having William Buckley as a secret agent."

"He probably thought you meant Elgin, Illinois."

"Why Elgin, Illinois?"

"Home of the Elgin watch factory."

"That's pronounced differently."

"I know," I said a little smugly, "my great-uncle owned it."

"I bet I know which side of the family he was on."

"How?" I said with a smile.

"I cannot see your Yankee relatives, between devastating whole forests of maple trees for syrup and running for elected office, also operating a watch factory in the midwest. It goes rather better on your father's side." He rubbed his fingers together like a modern-day Fagin.

"Don't be such a bigot."

"Me?" said McCandles dryly. "I'm just like your father— what is it he says?"

" 'Some of my best friends are Jews. Why, my wife's even married to one.' "

"Exactly."

"Well, is that the only news? What have you been up to?"

"I've been boring," McCandles said with a sigh. "Very, very boring. I get up in the morning and go eat cereal with lukewarm milk in Hall. I sit by myself except when Greenfield insists on telling me about the progress of his thesis and why he misses getting the *New York Times*. Since he's an orphan, he also goes on about his craving for parents."

"Is that interesting?"

"No—on all three counts. I think I've disabused him of the virtues of parents. Anyway, after breakfast I read the *Herald Tribune* and calculate how much more money I've lost in the stock market. Then I walk to Rhodes House and sit in the library. I open all the windows because the smell is so bad."

"You should try the PPE Reading Room."

"I have. It's got nothing on Rhodes House, believe me. Why don't the English bathe? In any case, I usually eat lunch with Newcastle, then I go back to Rhodes House for the afternoon. When I'm too bored to work I read all those journals from the fifty states. I now know more about commerce on the Great Lakes than anyone else at Oxford."

"I'm impressed."

"I can see you are. Finally, when I'm so bored I can't even read the *Arkansas Historical Review*, I walk back to my room and have a drink—a large drink. I eat dinner in Hall, call Audrey and try to cheer her up, then read a little and drink a lot more. I told you it was boring."

"You've convinced me now. We should have a party."

"Sarah Dominic's having one in London soon. But we may not be invited. She told Audrey she's not sure she can trust us to behave."

"I paid her for all those phone calls."

"Why is it that whenever you get drunk you start calling America?"

"Force of habit. I used to call Carol every week. It nearly bankrupted me."

"It's a peculiar kind of addiction."

"Well anyway, maybe we should have a party."

"In here?" McCandles looked disdainfully around my small quarters.

"At your place. We could get Eckstein to let us use his room."

"Great. Then we'd have to invite his friends. There would be our friends and twenty David Hockney types, feeling the curtains in German."

"There has to be something to do," I said. When he was in moods like this, McCandles could be exasperating. Nothing could relieve his boredom; all suggestions, ingenious or dull, were rejected with equal scorn.

"All last year I kept hoping my tutors would leave me alone," I continued. "Now that it's happened, I'm worried. I wish they'd pay me more attention."

"Actually," said McCandles seriously, "if you need entertainment, there is some tomorrow for free."

"What's that?"

"Lafayette Jackson's inaugural lecture. At Schools."

It was my turn to sound sarcastic. "Terrific. Why do I want to go hear Lafayette Jackson?"

"Because Newcastle will be there; I think it may be an interesting occasion. There's usually a question period and he's bound to ask some difficult ones."

"Why?"

"Didn't you hear about what happened when he went to see her?" When I shook my head he said, "That's right, I haven't told you about it."

"What happened?"

"It was a disaster." There was glee in McCandles' voice. "It was so typical of Newcastle; before seeing her he decided to do some research into her work. So he went and read her book, then he read all her articles in the *TLS* and *New York Review of Books.*"

"Oh God," I said with a groan.

"I couldn't believe it either. It took him three days. But he didn't merely read them, he checked them."

"What does *that* mean?"

"He researched her references, her *quotes.* Two hours before he was due to see her, he came over to me in the library and said he had found all sorts of mistakes, especially in her book. This island she said disappeared in an earthquake, well, according to Newcastle, it's not clear it even existed. He started showing evidence to me."

"Were they mistakes?"

"How should I know? He was so excited that I couldn't understand half of what he was saying."

"Why did he do all that?"

"Who knows? The boy's a walking model of pedantic research. If he'd ever apply those talents to his own work there'd be no stopping him. But the point is, he was supposed to see this woman about supervising his thesis. Instead he went and started pointing out all these 'mistakes' in her book."

"How did she react?"

"How do you think? At first, from what he's told me, she was just nonplussed. But, after a while, she clammed up. Newcastle told me it suddenly became apparent that she wasn't going to direct his thesis."

"What did he expect? You can't insult somebody and expect them to *help* you."

"Newcastle thinks he can. He came back from the interview and told me he wouldn't want her for a supervisor anyway. He said he had come to the conclusion that she was a fraud."

"Is she a fraud?"

"Probably," McCandles said indifferently. "Aren't they all?"

"But I thought she was very well known."

"It's been a recent rise to fame. George Arthur Newman liked her book, so suddenly everyone talks about her as the next Trevelyan."

"So what's Newcastle going to do? He's got to find a new adviser."

"I know, but all he's talking about now is 'exposing' Lafayette Jackson. That's why I thought you might want to come to her lecture."

I looked at the map on the wall. It was a map of precincts in the Detroit metropolitan area. I kept it there simply to distinguish myself from all the other Americans in England who immediately pasted phoney Hogarthian prints all over their walls. The hardest thing about liking England as much as I did was resisting the temptation to become ostentatiously Anglophile, with prints and teacups and an accent that sounded like the product of a harelip.

I said to McCandles, "You think Newcastle may be up to something?"

He responded in a fruity English voice: "I rather think he is. It will be *such* fun."

Three

⚜ *The next day* I had lunch with some distant relatives who were on an attenuated version of the Grand Tour—a day in Stratford, a day in Oxford, three hours in Devon, etc. They insisted on driving me out to the Trout, which they had read about in a guidebook. It is an awful place, overpriced and always crowded, and that day it was packed with loud and boozy Germans. We were forced to eat our salmon sandwiches crouching in a corner under one of the picturesque and obtrusive Tudor beams.

Still, my cousin—he was rising seventy but nonetheless my cousin—force-fed me several gin-and-tonics and I perked up after the first half hour's awkwardness. He was a retired lawyer who always wore soft and slightly rumpled Brooks Brothers suits; his wife was younger and a little breathless. "I never made it to college," she kept saying, as if this were like missing Jamaica on her last jaunt through the Caribbean. I had had more than my share of higher education by this point, and I assured her college was significantly overrated.

The conversation drifted pleasantly enough along these lines until my cousin, who was on my mother's side of the family, started praising Israel. They often do that, my mother's relatives, as if to show how much they've changed and how tolerant they've become. My stepgrandfather, long dead, was even worse. He was a crusty old shit whom I rather admired, but, although he'd once given eighty thousand dollars to the John Birch Society, he still felt compelled to praise the intellectual accomplishments of Jews whenever he saw my father.

After lunch, my cousin and his wife drove me back to town, and I gave them my half-hour tour of Oxford. As long as they get to see Wren's Tom Tower and the Magdalen deer park, visitors go away happy. I once escorted my father's aunt around my own favorite parts of Oxford—the lane lined by cherry trees that cuts next to Corpus Christi and runs down to the Meadow, the New College Gardens with the old city wall—and she subsequently wrote to my parents to complain that I hadn't shown her anything in the guidebooks. I'd learned my lesson and now kept strictly to the famous sights.

I said goodbye to my cousin and his wife at the Radcliffe Camera, then walked over to the High Street to look at the prints in Sanders' window until the time came to go hear Lafayette Jackson. I was standing in front of the shop when two familiar figures were reflected in the glass before me. Turning around I saw the short squat frame of Professor Hubert, Gladstone bag in hand, accompanied by Harry Sutro, an American who'd done graduate work at Oxford. Sutro taught somewhere in North Carolina now, either Davidson or Duke, but apparently he was back for a visit. He was tall and so thin as to be a masculine answer to anorexia, but at the moment his height was lessened by the bias to his walk (he moved forward in synch with Hubert's careful little steps) and by a pronounced tilt to his trunk so as better to hear his former tutor. Theirs was said to be a relationship of unbridled mutual affection, and much derided by McCandles and Newcastle. For Sutro's first book—a study of women in Congress based on his dissertation and supplementary interviews with the dwindling objects of his study—Hubert was known to have written a glowing and anonymous encomium in the *Economist*. So now with comedy in my heart, I shamelessly followed the odd couple down the High, enthralled by the Pisan slant of my countryman, until they reached Schools and I realized they, too, had come to praise Lafayette Jackson.

Inside, the lecture hall was not yet crowded. I spotted McCandles near the rear and joined him on the hard oak chairs the university provides to encourage rapt attention.

"Did you see Hubert and Sutro?" my friend asked with a snide smile.

"I followed them down from Sanders. What's Sutro doing here?"

"On sabbatical."

"Already? He's only been teaching a year."

"He received an NEH grant and UNC had to let him go."

"Jesus Christ," I exploded. "There's something very unjust about that."

"He is a prominent young political scientist," McCandles said with a deadpan expression.

"The hell he is. When I worked in New York last summer we got a review copy of his book. It was unreadable."

"Exactly what's wanted. If it were intelligible to an uneducated layman like yourself, Sutro's chances for tenure would be significantly reduced. As it is, I'd give him three to one he'll get tenure, even odds on a chair by the time he's forty. Possibly even Hubert's chair."

More people were entering the room, and McCandles pointed out the attending luminaries, who were, not surprisingly, of much the same appearance as the lesser-known. The seats filled up quickly like a tightly-packed egg carton, and I fought against the rising claustrophobia that events such as this induced. "Where's Newcastle?" I asked McCandles.

"I don't know. I've looked and looked, but I don't think he's here."

Quite suddenly, the murmur of voices ceased and the two back doors to the room were swung forward. In marched the Vice-Chancellor, clothed in an immense black gown with a red silk hood thrown arrogantly back over his shoulders. He was followed closely by a petite woman with short hair and enormous glasses. She, too, wore a gown, but it dwarfed her and hung in wavy folds all the way down to her black shoes. Finally, behind her by just a stride, came Newcastle, gownless in his faded green tweed jacket.

The procession moved down the middle aisle with speed. Members of the audience exchanged quick glances at the sight of Newcastle; when McCandles looked at me, I had to stifle an explosion of laughter. As the Vice-Chancellor neared the front of the room, he paused to let the woman behind him draw alongside before they both turned to sit in the two armchairs facing the audience. At this point, Newcastle suddenly veered to one side, visibly brushing against the woman, and sat down in the first row. There was a sweater draped along the chair's back; from its dingy orange color, I recognized it as his. Newcastle had already been in the room, it struck me, and reserved himself a seat. His astonishing entrance had been planned.

The Vice-Chancellor was a notorious alcoholic, given to prolix orations when the briefest remarks were in order. The audience stirred uneasily in anticipation as he stood up to speak, but he must have lunched soberly, for his words of introduction were inaudible and few. He sat down and Lafayette Jackson rose and moved to the lectern, a pink sheaf of pages clutched in her fist.

I whispered to McCandles. "Somehow I thought she would look different."

"I thought she was black," McCandles whispered back as she began to speak.

That was certainly part of my surprise, for instead of the formidable black woman I'd envisaged, there stood before the lectern one of Southern womanhood's more delicate flowers. Her skin was a pale sheet blotted only by a pink blush in each cheek. Her hands were tiny, marked by the thinnest of gold wedding bands. As she started to talk, I thought that even if I had never read "A Rose for Miss Emily," this is nonetheless how I would picture the heroine.

"It is an honor," she was saying hesitantly, "to give this lecture in what has so rightly been called an early home of history."

McCandles winced, and ahead I could see Newcastle shake his head. When I looked back several minutes later he was still shaking his head, slowly so that one could see just where the part in his hair had strayed. Lafayette Jackson had long since progressed past her mandatory note of thanks and was launched into her chosen topic—something to do with women slaves and higher education. To what then did Newcastle object? I nudged McCandles to point out our friend the Dissenter, and he raised his eyes and nodded to show that he had noticed, too. When after a few more minutes, Newcastle had still not ceased to shake his head, I had to stifle a laugh.

We were not alone in noticing that lonely head, which moved back and forth directly below the prim pair of hands gripping the rostrum. Professor Hubert was across the aisle from Newcastle, in the third row, and I could see his great moose eyes cast daggers at his wayward student. Soon other eyes followed, among them those of the Regius Professor. Yet Newcastle would have needed eyes in the back of his head to notice the disapproving scrutiny. Without them, he continued his own public rite of negation, occasionally interspersing his slow head shakes with the dramatic angst of Rodin's *Thinker,* clasping his forehead with the force of a vise.

It was not long before Ms. Jackson perceived the potent

impact of her words on at least one member of the audience. For a while, as she gamely read on, her eyes flickered perilously close to the jacketed figure below her, but, doubtless recalling the principle of stagecraft not to look at the audience, she was able to avoid the temptation and fixed her gaze firmly on some imagined Southern firmament. As she neared her conclusion, however, curiosity proved overwhelming and she gave way to a full long stare at the offender. I could hardly blame her. How Newcastle reacted to this I could not see but I can testify that his headshakes never wavered. For a moment Lafayette Jackson paused. Then drawing herself up to her inconsiderable height, she rapidly finished her speech. It was, I thought, a brave performance.

"Thank you very much," the Vice-Chancellor was saying before the applause had died completely. "I am certain members of the audience will find much to think about in your lecture, and I am certain, too, that they will now have many questions for you."

I was myself quite certain that I wasn't alone in giving a deep inward groan at this invitation, for it guaranteed another half-hour's imprisonment while various dim-witted graduate students showed off with recondite questions. There was no polite way to escape, given the Vice-Chancellor's remarks, so this made the sudden departure of Newcastle the more surprising. He strode out of the room with his shoulders hunched, looking at no one. It was an ostentatious exit, almost a slap at the Vice-Chancellor's plea for questions and the correlative suggestion that for a little while at least we should all stay put. McCandles turned to me with a look of mock-horror, then drew a finger rapidly across his throat.

That evening, I ate dinner at High Table, a termly privilege for "senior" students like myself with a B.A. already in hand. I had Mr. Hopkins on one side of me, but he talked throughout the meal with Quinn, the Irish biology don. From the country house novels I'd read, I thought that social prescription dictated a roughly equal division of one's attention at table to the guest on either side. But in my three or four experiences at High Table I had noticed that neither this nor any other nicety of manners was observed. Indeed, the furies of academic politics were translated wholesale to High Table, with much parading of snubs, cynical interjections, and contemptuous dismissals, all flowing freely in the four-course structure of a guest night meal.

On my other side I found Krattenstein, another senior student like myself, and I talked with him throughout dinner. He was a Montreal Jew, heavy-set, with thick hands and a receding hairline. He was a quiet presence in College and worked each day in the Bodleian Library, studiously amassing facts about England's relations with Canada in the Second World War. He was moral (although not moralistic) and cautious, considering everything in such careful assessments that his conversation appeared humorless. Deeply Zionist, he knew we differed on Israel's politics, yet he seemed content to leave our differences alone. Slow to anger, he was nevertheless formidable when offended, and the dons respected him, not least because of an insult he'd offered the Master in his first term in College. The Master was an ex-Foreign Service Officer and fiercely pro-Arab. He also drank heavily, a practice which would fortify his anti-Zionist tilt. On one occasion he began claiming that Jews should be banned from the Foreign Service because of their inevitable dual feelings of nationality. Krattenstein, who had said nothing until then, suddenly asked coldly, "What about alcoholics? They also have dual affections: for Britain and for Bottle." The Master never spoke to him again.

This evening there were no such *bons mots*. We ate avocados and prawns with a sweet Rhine wine. The Dean, ostentatiously oenophilic, complained loudly about the wine and

German wines in general. The entrée—a mixed grill with tomatoes and mushrooms—was accompanied by a Burgundy that pacified the Dean. Throughout the courses, Krattenstein was boringly well-behaved, telling me about his work in excessive detail; I retaliated by telling him about Lafayette Jackson's lecture and Newcastle's performance.

"That's extraordinary!" We were eating the *coeurs à la crème* by then and at first I thought he was referring to the dessert. Then he added, "I mean, it's such gross rudeness that I can only assume this fellow must be very self-destructive."

I shrugged. "It was goddamned funny, I can tell you that. His adviser was there and you should have seen his face."

"Did Newcastle know he was there?"

"He must have. The whole History Faculty attended."

Krattenstein said, "Then he must be *very* disturbed."

"This woman Jackson seemed to take it in stride for the most part. In a way, that made Newcastle's performance even stranger. Hilarious, actually."

"Come off it," Krattenstein said impatiently. "There's clearly something wrong with him. He may have sacrificed his whole career with that little display."

Krattenstein struck me as unduly serious about Newcastle's behavior, so I talked about something else. We left Hall together and went for port and nuts in the Senior Common Room. When the port came around a second time, Hopkins deigned to talk to me and arranged to go over my paper on Russell and Wittgenstein. All thoughts of Lafayette Jackson and Newcastle disappeared at the prospect of finally nailing down The Theory of Types.

Four

It was about two weeks later that I made my way to Rhodes House Library, in search of McCandles and the latest American magazines. I was accustomed to studying in spurts, propelled only by the approach of a tutorial, and had no fixed place for work. I was writing poems at the time, none of them very good, and this I did in the new law library, where I would requisition one of the faculty tables in the back with a view of several playing fields. Light reading I did in my room or the college library. Course assignments led me to the Merton Street Philosophy Library or the PPE Reading Room. Mine was an eclectic and undemanding schedule, made less demanding still by the deceptively benign requirements of the system.

I found a mountainous array of books where McCandles usually sat and a mess of yellow legal sheets inscribed with his small, neat calligraphy. He could not have gone far, for his bag was under the table. A deep red bookbag with a stencilled hammer and sickle, it was a souvenir from his tour of Russia the year before. McCandles swore he was going to take it back to his Louisiana hometown and parade it proudly down Main Street.

A copy of the *TLS* lay half-submerged on McCandles'

desk, so I sat down in his chair to read it until his return. I read a long review about Auden, three obscure bibliographical pieces by someone named Geoffrey Naylor, then I turned to the letters page. It was rarely as interesting as the correspondence in the *Spectator*, but occasionally two scholars would erupt in battle, assuming that the *pro forma* bows to professional courtesy which began their letters somehow tempered the full-fledged malice which then emerged. This particular issue did not disappoint me. Halfway down the second column, as the third letter printed, I found the following:

Sir,

In her lengthy analysis of prison literature Lafayette Jackson has made the following errors:

She writes of "Leavenworth, America's first great prison . . . "—it was not. By virtually any standard of prison "greatness," that honor must go to Sing Sing, built in 1824, or its smaller predecessor, Auburn (1817).

She writes of "my native South, where the overwhelming majority of prisoners remain black." Native or not, she is in error. According to D. Tourwald Parker's *Census of American Prisons* (Padducah, Kentucky: 1973), it is only in federal prisons in the South that blacks predominate. If we count state prisons, city gaols, and other forms of parochial incarceration, the ratio of blacks to whites is in fact roughly equal, and less unbalanced than in any other region of the country, except for California.

Third and last, Ms. Jackson concludes her analysis with a quotation from what she calls a Southern "folk blues": "I was set free after twenty years behind bars, but prison's the only life I know." This fragment, although doubtless moving in its way, may lose some of its force when its origins are revealed. It is in fact from the song "Prisoner's Lament," composed by W. S. Gilbert shortly after the severance of relations with Mr. Sullivan. Its lines may well be read with a psychological bias that discerns the presence of a metaphor about Mr. Gilbert's feelings towards his former collaborator. But it would take rather more than mere psychological speculation to apply Gilbert's charming lyrics to the manacles and rock blasts of a Georgian chain gang.

Yours faithfully,

P. R. C. Newcastle
Christ Church, Oxford

I especially liked the "P. R. C.," which made Newcastle sound vaguely liturgical in the holiest of Oxford colleges. The bit about Gilbert was pretty clever, too.

A voice came over my shoulder. "I want to make Xeroxes—thousands of them—and send them all to the University of Maryland."

"Why Maryland?" I asked as McCandles' face came into view.

"That's where Lafayette Jackson teaches."

"This is devastating," I said, pointing to the *TLS*.

"I'd say so."

"How did he find all these errors? What does he know about prison literature?"

"Next to nothing. But he read all the books she reviewed, and then some. Look." McCandles pointed across the room. I craned my head and saw Newcastle in a far corner, scribbling away furiously with one hand, picking his nose rather less energetically with the other.

"What's he doing?"

McCandles laughed. "Working on her next piece. When he went to see her she made the mistake of telling him the name of some new book she's reviewing."

"For the *TLS*?"

"Worse, for the *New York Review of Books*. Newcastle's not only read the book, he's digging around in the field for ammunition."

"Is that what he's doing over there now?"

"I'm sure it is. Let's go see." McCandles motioned me to get up and follow him and I did. We walked over to Newcastle's corner of the room, ignoring the stares of more serious students. McCandles had nicknames for the grimmest of them, and I noticed "Miss Germany"—a blonde blue-eyed Rhodes Scholar with a cretinous tilt to her lips—making notes on file cards on the desk nearest Newcastle. As we confronted our prey, Miss Germany looked over at us and frowned.

"Hello," said Newcastle coldly, unhappy to be interrupted. He had *The Journal of Central American Studies* on the desk before him, and a catalogue from a New Orleans book dealer.

"Time for tea," McCandles sang out in an upper class falsetto. A loud sh-sh-sh swept down at us from the librarian's desk at the far end.

"Come on," said McCandles less formally, and with some hesitation Newcastle followed us out of the library. We walked out of the front entrance of Rhodes House, well beneath its crowning Zimbabwe bird, through the domed memorial room and the chiselled names of fallen Rhodes Scholars on the walls. McCandles performed a small dance on the memorial seal while I pretended not to be embarrassed. "There should be a room," McCandles declared as we swung open the great front door, "with the names of the victims of Rhodes Scholars. Thousands of people from all over the globe, bored to death by the self-importance of the elect."

Crossing Parks Road, we bought tea in cheap white cups in the Science Building Common Room. It was a room of quite incredible squalor, painted gray and furnished in sporadic clusters of garishly-painted plastic chairs. It was early enough in the afternoon to be uncrowded.

"So," said McCandles as he sat down carefully on a cracked orange chair.

"So," I said as I perched on an equally fragile seat.

"What do you mean?" asked Newcastle irritably, scratching a small pimple on his upper lip. He looked even less comfortable in his chair than the two of us.

"So how's your work going?" McCandles asked. I thought this an unusual question since McCandles usually hated to talk shop, unless it was to disparage Hubert or another of his teachers.

"Very well, thank you," said Newcastle seriously. "I've found some very interesting things."

"Really," I said politely, hoping I wouldn't have to hear another account of why he couldn't find any Carolina antebellum abolitionists. "Do you always work in Rhodes House?"

"That's where my material is, though not the books on Central America."

"Central America?" I asked in some wonder. I noticed McCandles was smiling.

"Yes, and South America as well. I've just read Birmingham's account of the last days of Che. Would you think it fair to say that Che's appeal to American youth equalled that of H. Rap Brown?"

Newcastle's parallels were always odd, but this seemed to me to go too far. "I wouldn't have said either had much pull among the American youth I know," I answered.

"Really now?" Newcastle did not seem discomfited by my response. "Where did you go to university?"

"Yale."

"Ah," he said slowly and sarcastically as if this explained everything.

"So tell us about Central America," McCandles demanded.

I looked at him with a puzzled expression but he cheerfully ignored me.

"Well," said Newcastle cautiously, "I really just have to wait and see. I imagine her piece is due out any day now. I think I'm well prepared."

"Well prepared for what?"

"For anything that stupid bitch Lafayette Jackson has to say."

There was a sudden venomous quality to his voice I found disturbing. "Why are you worried about her?" I asked. "I thought she didn't want to supervise your thesis."

This was tactless on my part, but Newcastle seemed impervious. "She doesn't," he replied briskly, "and from what I've discovered about her work I'm very glad of that. What I can't understand is why Oxford invited her. I'm sure if they knew about the serious improprieties in her work they would rescind their invitation."

"I doubt it," said McCandles. "It's a little late for that."

"Is that what your letter in the *TLS* is all about?" I asked with a laugh. "To make Oxford rescind its invitation?"

Newcastle grew haughty. "Partly," he said solemnly. "But if Oxford can't recognize its mistake, at least other institutions may do so."

"You should send a copy of your letter to her department chairman in Maryland," I said sarcastically.

"Possibly," he answered in all seriousness. He lifted his cup and drank the rest of his tea in one long swallow. Then he carefully wiped his lips with the back of his hand. The effect was of fastidious seediness. "Now I must get back to my work," Newcastle announced. He bid hasty farewells and departed.

"Do you want another cup of tea?" McCandles asked me.

"Christ no. Let's get out of this place; it's horrible."

McCandles wasn't keen to return immediately to Rhodes

House, so we walked along until we came to the Broad, already teeming with the cars and buses of the early tourists. We paused in front of Blackwell's and looked at the titles in the window. "I love Blackwell's," I said. "I could buy a book here every day."

"I do," said McCandles lugubriously. "Here, or at the antiquarian division on Ship Street." McCandles had a passion for rare books that I shared in energy but not expenditure. "Did you know that it's moving?" he added.

"No, where to?"

"Miles away. You'll need a car to get there."

"Audrey will take you." She had a car, an old Morris.

"I suppose so. But the antiquarian store was one of the few places I liked to go when Audrey wasn't around and I was bored."

"You're always bored, Wilmarth."

"I know. So are you, you just don't recognize the fact."

"Maybe." I saw Krattenstein across the street, slowly climbing the Sheldonian steps on his way to the Bodleian. I felt vaguely hungry. "Is Newcastle doing any of his own work?"

"None. He spends all his time reading whatever Lafayette Jackson's writing about."

"That's pretty strange."

"Whoever said Newcastle was normal? You would prefer the sanity, the stability of—let's say—young Krattenstein?" McCandles must also have seen the Canadian head for the library. "For all his eccentricity, Newcastle's one of the few even remotely interesting people around here."

"Eccentric is a mild way of describing him. I think he's one of the creepiest people I know."

"Maybe," said McCandles indifferently. "Thank God Bicker's coming back soon."

"When?" Bicker was interesting and a friend of us both.

"Next week. He's supposed to give a talk in Nuffield."

"Oh." I stared at the window display. They were exhibiting only philosophy texts, including a book on Frege by Hopkins.

"What's today?" McCandles asked.

"Thursday."

"I thought so. Listen, do you want to go to London?"

"Maybe. When?"

"Tomorrow. I have to go to a History Faculty party at four. Why don't you come by there around five and we can take the train in? I'd skip the party but I promised Hubert I'd be there. He seems to set great store by his students' attendance at functions."

"Where would we stay?" I really meant where would I stay, since McCandles stayed with Audrey.

"Sarah's. We could see a play or go gambling."

"I thought I was on Sarah's blacklist."

"Not quite. Anyway, she's away for a week so her place is empty. Just don't get drunk and start calling America again. Audrey will fix it up."

Five

✖ *The History Faculty* party was in the Balliol Junior Common Room. I packed a small overnight bag and walked up from college to collect McCandles · before we caught the train to London. I had intended to beckon him from the Common Room door, but the place was thick with students and dons, and I had to wade through the crowd to find him. Thin clouds of cigarette smoke trailed through the air like strings of cotton candy, and an assortment of plastic cups sticky with cheap sherry littered the few tables. Alcohol in Britain is sufficiently expensive that the greatest social magnet—greater than girls, or food, or drugs—is a free drink.

I saw McCandles at last, listening with feigned politeness as Hubert rattled away. As I drew near, I could see Lafayette Jackson standing next to McCandles with a similar expression of courteous inattention on her face. She was slightly taller than my friend but still on the short side. She was wearing a fawn-colored Marks and Spencer's twinset and pearls; I recognized the outfit because Audrey, McCandles' fiancée, had made fun of an identical sweater and cardigan combination the week before as we walked through that shop. "Can you imagine buying *that*?" Audrey had asked me then, and looking at Lafayette now, I realized Audrey had no future in retailing.

Worried lest Lafayette Jackson become aware of my scrutiny, I fell to studying the sensible black Mary Janes and stockings bunched at the ankle that completed her demure ensemble. Her right hand held a small bag of light vanilla leather; in her other hand she clutched a full glass of sherry. Her face was as pink as the day she lectured, but the flush to her cheeks could not be alcohol-induced, I concluded, since she took only timid sips from her glass. She used powder freely on her nose, in the undisguised fashion of middle-aged women, but I did not put her age at over forty-five. Unmarked by mascara or eyeshadow, her eyes were oddly, almost ghostly pale, with the thinnest of browlines. Her mouth was small with puffy, ever-so-slightly chapped lips, and her chin was rounded like the bulbous end of a pear. Finally, I looked at her hair, which was cut short, in boyish half-inch mousey curls that reminded me of a late Roman emperor, androgynous and soft.

Examination of this dowdy spectacle left me even more perplexed. It was in this small figure of a woman that New-castle was investing his energies, his animus? In this that McCandles and I had laughed so hard? Looking at the woman I felt simultaneously a mild aversion and a somewhat stronger sympathy. My response was conditioned at first, I suppose, by youth's contempt for plainness, then by comparison of Lafayette with the women of my own family, who are, without exception, direct, formidable, handsome, and tough. If my female relatives were at the sharp end of the spice rack— peppercorns, sea salt, oregano—Lafayette Jackson was the blandest of lemon verbena. I somehow felt she needed taking care of.

My thoughts returned to the difficulty of extricating McCandles from his conversation with Hubert in time to catch our train. The problem was partly solved when McCandles turned in my direction, then gestured me to join him.

I shook hands with Hubert, who poured me a glass of sherry and turned back to McCandles, resuming a short lecture on the iniquities of Reconstruction. I was left to make my own introduction to Lafayette Jackson, who seemed quietly relieved to listen to someone else.

"You're American?" she asked, and when I nodded she said softly, "There seem to be an awful lot of us here." Her accent was mildly but distinctly Southern. There was a wistful intonation to her voice that, I came to realize, reflected no conscious attitude on her part towards anything she said, but that, nonetheless, colored all her remarks with the pathos of a far older woman.

"Oxford's full of Americans," I said genially. "But you'll find we can be avoided if you try. It varies from college to college. Some take lots of Americans, others won't have anything to do with us."

She nodded so seriously at this that I felt a little silly for making such a lofty generalization. She asked me which college I belonged to; when I told her she displayed a disproportionate enthusiasm. "How lucky for you," she gushed. "I think it's one of the very nicest colleges." My college is certainly old, and usually receives half a dozen lines of commentary in any given guidebook, but it rarely evinces more than modest approval. "Yes," Lafayette cooed, repeating the name of my college, "it and Magdalen are my very favorites," thus linking grand to diminutive in a definitive example of bathos.

"Well," I said doubtfully, "I'm sure there are Fellows in my college who would give anything to have you repeat that." When she looked at me curiously, I changed tack. "Are you here in Oxford long?"

"Just this term. And maybe part of July. My appointment's only for one term. Actually," and she giggled shyly, "I'm only obliged to deliver a single lecture and I've already given that. But there's so much to see I know I won't have time to visit it all."

"There are a lot of colleges," I conceded. "Not to mention the countryside. Have you been out in the country at all? There're some beautiful villages nearby."

"Oh yes," she said deeply, "we had the nicest time last weekend. We took a drive through the Cotswolds and visited a friend of ours. He's a bookseller and lives in a little cottage near Broadway."

"A bookseller," I said with interest, and since virtually anything interesting tends to make me leave my manners behind, I asked forwardly who it was she had visited.

"A man named Malcolm Allison. Do you know him?"

I shook my head. "Not personally. But I've certainly heard of him." It did not take a bibliophile to know of Malcolm Allison, for although he had a considerable reputation as a collector of late Latin verse, he was better known as a surviving member of the Oxford Aesthetes of the 1920s. Allison's memoirs, recently published, recounted in great and self-important detail his intimacy with Harold Acton, Maurice Bowra, Evelyn Waugh, and lesser lights of the period. Oddly enough, none of their memoirs mentioned him.

But I stayed silent as Lafayette Jackson praised the comforts of Allison's Cotswold cottage, the charms of his garden ("Roses everywhere!" she exclaimed), the beauty of the William Morris wallpaper (reproductions I felt certain). "What a kind man," she concluded with a sigh.

"Do you collect books yourself?"

"Not really," she said with a smile, "but I know some booksellers in America. There's one in New Orleans in particular—he's a great friend of my husband—who seems to know every antiquary dealer in England. He wrote off to so many of them on my behalf that I expect all our free time this spring will be spent in bookshops."

"Really?" I said, thinking that McCandles would be interested in this. He was constantly being frustrated by the reclusive snobbery of English dealers, particularly in London, where his accent seemed to suggest to them that he was intent only on cadging another relic for the University of Texas. I looked over at McCandles to try to draw him into the conversation but he was busy helping Hubert open a recalcitrant bottle of sherry. They both twisted and twisted again the bottle's screw cap to no avail. When Hubert looked away for further assistance, McCandles suddenly took the bottle in his mouth and with a savage chomp pulled away the cap. As Hubert turned back, McCandles handed him the opened bottle with a decorous smile.

"Have you been to London to see any dealers?" I asked.

Lafayette Jackson nodded and recited a fairly standard list of eminent names—Quaritch, Maggs, Rota. Then, as if leaving the best for last, she said that she had especially enjoyed visiting Samuel Goodiston, a contact through her husband's friend Smiley, the New Orleans dealer.

Goodiston, that shyster, I thought to myself, surprised to hear his name invoked in the company of more distinguished and infinitely more honest dealers. I suppressed a cynical smile and decided to change the subject. "I went to your lecture," I said slowly. "I enjoyed it very much." I refrained from citing the reasons for my enjoyment.

"You're kind to say so," she said with the excessive long 'i' of the Southerner. "I was fairly nervous," she added. "I'm glad someone thought it went well."

"Yes indeed," I said politely. It struck me that I was giving a poor imitation of a patronizing don, but I find it difficult to respond to sincerity. "Tell me, where do you teach in the States?"

"Maryland."

"Are you from there?"

"No," she said softly. "I was raised in South Carolina."

"Your family is here, too?" I realized I was asking questions almost automatically, perhaps to hide my own unease. It was a useful habit when I worked as a journalist; less attractive now that I'd left the profession.

"Yes," she said with a polite smile. "My husband came over with me."

"Is he a professor, also?"

"No, he's a banker. They gave him leave so he could join me."

"How nice. Are your children with you or did they stay in the States?"

"We don't have any children," she said shyly, making me feel guilty for assuming she had. "Not yet anyway." Lafayette Jackson looked beyond child-bearing age to me, and this thought must have shown in my face for she added in a whisper, "We're hoping to adopt a child."

"Back in the States?"

"Yes," she said proudly. "We're trying to adopt a little Vietnamese boy. One of the 'boat children.'"

I did not know what to say to this. Handy at inspiring confidences on short acquaintance, I am not equally adept at responding to them once they are imparted. It seemed clear to me that for all her stillness (a trait I usually take for hidden, inner strength), Lafayette Jackson was at sea here at an Oxford party. She seemed quite out of her depth—whatever her reputation—yet it was I, fumbling for the appropriate response, who was in danger of drowning.

Hubert saved me. That he had heard any of what Lafayette Jackson had told me so quietly surprised me, but he certainly heard enough to interject himself. "You sail?" he said loudly to Lafayette Jackson.

She blushed deeply. "I beg your pardon?"

"I heard a mention of boats," Hubert said confidently. "I

thought perhaps you were talking about sailing." When he
saw the blank looks on our faces he said by way of explanation, "I'm very keen on sailing. I thought perhaps coming
from Maryland," he pronounced it to rhyme with Fairyland,
"you did some sailing, too. Chesapeake Bay, what?" Hubert
was the only Englishman I have ever encountered who said
"what" in the Wodehousian manner.

This was the perfect opportunity for escape. McCandles
raised his eyes at me and we each carefully executed a backwards two-step and retreated slowly towards the door, leaving
Hubert one-on-one with Lafayette Jackson. Hubert was so
engrossed in a recital of yawls he had known that we slipped
away unnoticed.

Outside we walked in double-time towards the station.
"You might have warned me," I complained as we moved
down George Street. "I would have met you at the station
if I'd known I was in for that."

"It serves you right," McCandles said emphatically. "It
should teach you to praise God you're not a graduate student.
I know how you think, how you envy me most of the time.
You have to write an essay every week—two if you're not
careful—brownnose your tutors, and worry about exams.
'McCandles,' you think bitterly, 'he has it soft. Only a senes-
cent adviser to worry about and the small matter of a thesis.'
But now you know. I say it serves you right."

"At least you *know* Hubert," I protested. "I'd never met
that woman before, I didn't have the faintest idea what to
talk to her about." And then I added with gratuitous cruelty,
"She's not exactly Maryland's answer to Madame de Staël."

"It wouldn't make any difference to me if she were," said
McCandles as we neared Blackwell's business offices. They
are housed in a black-green glass shell that looks like the
Miesian product of a week when the master left his glasses
at home. "As a graduate student," McCandles went on

grandly, "let me tell you one home truth: it doesn't matter which luminary you're talking to, it never pays to check their wattage." He paused. "Or was she really that dim?"

"Not dim, just earnest. Very nice, but very earnest. Earnest and almost staggeringly naive. She knows a lot of booksellers, though."

"I'm not surprised. Newcastle told me as much."

"He did?"

"Yes. He thinks he's onto something." McCandles scoffed. "You know Newcastle. Everything in the woman you took for innocence he sees as doubly devious—the mask of a virgin hiding the rancid heart of a whore."

"Come on," I said at the triteness of the metaphor.

"That's not me talking," McCandles said defensively. "It's Newcastle. He claims the correspondence Lafayette published in her book all came from a New Orleans dealer, someone named Smiley. Smiley also sold Oxford a collection of Robert E. Lee papers that Newcastle is half-convinced is phony."

"She mentioned Smiley. But how did Newcastle find this out?" We were passing the Royal Oxford Hotel, a plain structure of Clipsham stone that looked like yellowing concrete, and a suitable introduction to the grotesque Deco Gothic of Nuffield College behind it.

"Hard work mainly," said McCandles, "and a series of letters to American bookdealers—including Smiley—pretending to be a wealthy British collector of 19th century Americana."

"Jesus," I said appreciatively. "He makes me feel sorry for the woman."

"Sorry for Lafayette Jackson? For God's sake, why? She has a chair at Maryland and the prestige of an Oxford visiting appointment. What does Newcastle have? Plenty of brains, diligence we know, and a social manner that means anyone would dread having dinner with him, much less elect him to a fellowship. You should be sorry for *him*. Besides, weren't you just complaining how boring the woman is?"

I shrugged. "Boring, but nice. I can't believe she'd do anything fraudulent."

It was McCandles' turn to act noncommital. As usual, he broke this ambivalent mood with an exultant whoop. His conversation had a special sensitivity to potential impasse, and would move deftly along tangential lines to a more established source of interest. "*God, it was funny!*" he exclaimed.

"What was so funny?"

"I'm not sure which was the funnier," he said carefully, "Hubert's misunderstanding or the idea of that woman adopting a Vietnamese orphan."

"What do you mean?," I said slowing down by the taxis parked outside the station. There had been nothing impressive about Lafayette Jackson, to be sure, but somehow her proposed adoption of a "boat child" struck me as admirable, if not the sort of thing I planned to do myself.

McCandles sensed this reaction in me, for he said impatiently, "Oh, come off it. Can't you see anything funny in that woman bringing up an Asian child in Maryland? My aunt talked about adopting one, too, but my aunt's crazy. She just wanted one to be her slave. She's always complaining that she never gets to live like her ancestors did."

This did make me laugh. There was a frankly unreconstructed style to McCandles' family that I found disarming after so much media advocacy of a "New South." "Well anyway," I said, "she seems a perfectly straightforward woman to me. I can't understand what Newcastle has against her. Even if she likes Samuel Goodiston."

"What's wrong with that?" McCandles asked perversely, since he had been the one to tell me of that dealer's notoriety.

"Oh, come on," I said impatiently. "Carling at Blackwell's

even told me Goodiston had changed his name. It used to be Goldstein."

"So what? Lots of people do that," said McCandles blithely, trying further to inflame me. I think he found my diffidence about Lafayette Jackson annoying, but I decided not to give in to his counteroffensive. So I said, "Not in my father's family."

"I thought they were so assimilated," McCandles said tauntingly. "No Chanukkah, no Israeli war bonds."

"I suppose so," I said as we bought our tickets and walked to the platform. "But the one thing none of them ever does is change their name. Why, my grandfather," I said expansively, since a loudspeaker announced that the train was running late, "had a friend named Rosenberg. They used to play golf together, with a bunch of other German Jews, at a country club outside Detroit. One year Rosenberg moved to Kansas City—this was just before the war—and used the occasion to change his name to Ross. About a year later my grandfather and his other golfing cronies sent 'Ross' a telegram." I waited for McCandles' response.

"What did it say?" he said with some interest.

" 'Welcome to ye olde order of the Ancient Caledonian Clan of Ross,' and was signed 'in a spirit of Gaelic amity—Benny Ross, Abie Ross, Hymie Ross, Sidney Ross, and Mo Ross.' "

McCandles laughed in delight.

"So don't tell me how wonderful Goodiston is," I said sternly. "I know a phony when I see one."

Six

❄ *I had first* met McCandles through the offices of Andrew Mercy, a genuine lunatic. Like McCandles, Mercy was from the South, but where this feature glowed around my friend like a kind of cultural nimbus, Mercy's Southern-ness glared like a loud necktie.

Mercy and I fell in together, for when I first arrived at Oxford he was the only other American in my college, although a year ahead of me. Naturally, on any occasion in which nationality became conspicuous—conversation on a point of politics, a discussion of accents—Mercy and I were lumped together as "the Americans." Given this involuntary association, it seemed best that we should get along, and for a time at least we did.

But we had nothing in common, coming from different parts of the States, nursing different interests and ambitions. Mercy was an ex-chemistry student now reading law; not so secretly, he wanted to be Governor of Georgia. I was a former English major studying philosophy and politics in the dim hope these disciplines might keep me out of the journalism career I had already begun before coming to Oxford. I found Mercy's political ambitions banal; doubtless, he felt the same about my vaguer aspirations.

At first, Mercy and I drank together most evenings, and we would do our best to make conversation. I think it was Mercy's passion for the South that kept our friendship from fraying sooner than it did, for when Mercy's intense chauvinism first revealed itself I felt my interest in him rise. Fanaticism intrigues me; it always has. Yet Mercy's manifesto remained a mystery to me; and as winter approached, I slowly came to realize that to understand a Southerner you had to be one.

McCandles was indisputably Southern—so much so that the strength of his credentials unnerved Andrew Mercy, who had the misfortune of a midwestern mother. There is no fanaticism so great or so defensive as that of the *arriviste* partisan. But this difference between McCandles and Mercy was not originally apparent to me; when I would drop into Mercy's room to find McCandles there, I was ignorant of the social and historical tensions that afflict the South as much as others do England. Instead, I merely felt like an outsider as the two talked constantly about "home," and my slight discomfort was magnified by Mercy's satisfaction that I was beyond the pale. You'd have thought I was spending time with an unbending Jesuit skeptical of converts and thus especially gratified by the improbability of my admission to the order.

Only slowly did it dawn on me that McCandles did not share Mercy's regional obsession. For one thing, he had a sense of humor, of farce really, a malicious appreciation of the ridiculous. This was conspicuously lacking in the earnest temperament of Andrew Mercy. And although McCandles was genetically Southern in a way that Mercy was not, he nonetheless retained, in the manner of the socially-conscious aristocrat, a skeptical sense of his inheritance.

In this ambiguity, McCandles and I were very much alike; more specifically, we each had fathers in love with a pose, an elaborated disguise which, though constantly refined, fooled no one. Thus McCandles' father played the aristocratic landowner, ignorant of books, conversant only with shotguns, bird dogs, and rural blacks. Five minutes with the man, as I discovered when he visited his son during that first Oxford year, gave the game away; when he disappeared briefly in Blackwell's, McCandles and I found him upstairs, furtively purchasing a Tacitus translation. It was more than the text that brought home the parallels with my own father, who, having taught Vergil to freshmen in Michigan each autumn for thirty years, professed no interest from September through November in anything more heroic than the limits on small game bags and steelhead leaders. My father's main pleasure from his sons derived from our ignorance of his professional pursuits—"Arma virumque cano" was the start *and* finish of my classical education.

If this similarity of paternal behavior seems too obscure to account for the closeness of my friendship with McCandles, there were other, more obvious bonds. We had both been to boarding school and college in the east, and in prep school we had both felt outsiders and hated it. We both liked books and were reasonably athletic as well—McCandles was an even better skeet shot than his father—yet both of us viewed exercise as the puerile ethos of prep schools everywhere, a conceit to be avoided. We adhered to the old dictum that when any urge for physical activity stirred we should promptly lie down for a rest, large whiskey at hand, until the madness passed.

McCandles' mother was an alcoholic; mine an invalid; so we had each been raised by the stern hand of powerful fathers and, more curiously, by large, maternal black women. From an early age we were thus familiar with the starch-heavy diet of the black South: while McCandles in Louisiana gnawed at spareribs and corn, I sat in Ann Arbor tucking into fried chicken and passing up the collard greens. Each of us (I as the family's youngest, he as an especially small child) first witnessed the world from a hiding place behind a black woman's skirts. In this "pre-formative" stage, the perspective was secure and confidence-inspiring; it was an incredibly alien vantage point as well. Derailed from the more obvious patterns of parentage, we were nevertheless superficially normal.

Yet in us both lurked, I think, an emotional want of some kind that little in life seemed to mollify. Whatever was missing, only the dramatic could supply—preferably tragicomedy. Catastrophes were especially of interest, preceded only by our joint passion for the ludicrous, the eccentric, even the insane. My own interest grew slowly, nurtured by a strong streak of eccentricity in my family that was embarrassing to my parents and thus an endless source of fascination for me. McCandles had seemingly been born with a cynic's delight in lunacy and disaster. If there were a heart soft as putty beating somewhere beneath his adamantine exterior, I never found it.

Our mutual attachment to life's *bizarreries* might never have surfaced (and we might never have become such good friends) had we not had the spectacle of Andrew Mercy's unravelling to unite us. All winter, Mercy grew stranger, his fanaticism deepening as the English rain each day soaked his talk of peaches, pussy, and the new Confederacy. My attempts to widen the scope of conversation were dismissed by Mercy, who no longer cared even to compare his alien English surroundings with the monotonously dwelled-upon environs of the South. Even McCandles grew tired of this, and one night as we left Mercy's room together he said as much to me.

Interested that my own boredom was shared by someone I'd taken to be a partisan of the Southern party line, I bought McCandles a beer in the graduate common room. The crack

I'd discerned in Southern unity soon widened to a fissure as we laughed at Mercy's regional mania, his unrelenting gravity. We laughed more when Mercy suddenly came into the common room, saw us both there and left abruptly. There was a paranoid glint in his eyes.

After that, my relations with Mercy grew stilted. I had never felt close to him and so at first made little of his gradual coolness, which was in any case more pronounced in his attitude towards McCandles. When the three of us gathered in Mercy's room palpable tension set in; I found myself talking solely to McCandles while Mercy watched us with beady suspicion. Soon our meetings grew less frequent and when McCandles stopped going to Mercy's room altogether, Mercy voiced the feelings of distrust I had sensed. McCandles had betrayed the South, Mercy said tersely. Betrayed the what? I asked. The South, Mercy repeated. I shook my head in disbelief as Mercy explained this. It was more, clearly, than a matter of letting down the side, or lapsing forgivably from duty's path; no, McCandles had deserted a cause, a creed, an ethic, by which Andrew Mercy lived. Had not McCandles gone to a Northern boarding school, a Northern college, a second university abroad? Would he not now attend law school in the North, instead of in Louisiana where he belonged? A certain straying could be forgiven, but this was heresy in full revolt.

Well, I thought to myself as I left Mercy after these curious declarations, the poor guy is under strain—he has his finals soon and would be leaving Oxford, perhaps his mother's ill, something must be eating him. But Mercy's warped conviction of McCandles' "betrayal" did not subside; instead it grew deeper; it mushroomed into hate. It was, I see now, a class hatred; that of the sharecropper, chomping on local tobacco, for the cosmopolitan aristocrat who wore English linen and sat on furniture shipped south from Boston. But the expressed motive for his hate—McCandles' treachery—never made sense and still doesn't.

Soon Mercy and I were not friends either, although I was exempt from the charges. The problem was that I continued to be friendly with McCandles, talking with him when I met him in the street and once having another beer with him in my college common room. Somehow, Mercy knew this, and took the next opportunity to confront me with what he interpreted as my infidelity. There was something oddly passionate in his reproach, and something creepy, too, as if for all his talk of girls Mercy cared most about his male relationships. Mercy informed me I could not expect to be his friend if I were also McCandles'. I made it clear I didn't expect it at all.

Mercy's behavior was loony enough that McCandles and I discussed it gleefully whenever we saw each other. Mercy I saw only infrequently, passing him by the Porter's Lodge, for he was studying hard for his Finals in law. The full extent of his emotional disturbance was revealed finally at the Kentucky Derby party given in Magdalen by Cantucci—the creepy shyster who had been savaged by skinheads. His party was a lavish affair; the invitation said "Creative Fancy dress," and my own and McCandles' invitations were secured only by Cantucci's ignorance of our common disdain for him. There was frank hypocrisy to our contempt, since neither McCandles nor I would ever want our animosities to result in social isolation. And Cantucci was not a malicious person, merely a very pretentious one. His father was a cocktail bar pianist in Des Moines; not perhaps a thing to boast about in the jumped-up social life of Americans at Oxford, but hardly a matter for secrecy and shame. Cantucci usually told people his father was in banking.

But the pianist's son could sure give a party, and on that bright Saturday afternoon in May I arrived in Magdalen to find a marquee erected between the Old Quad and the New Buildings. There was a small combo playing bad Dixieland jazz, oysters served from a barrel, and half a dozen cases of surprisingly good fizzy white wine. A mixed crowd of Americans milled around the tent, decked in blazers and ducks, smart outfits from Saks, boaters and bright hats. I hate fancy dress and came in a grey suit, a red carnation my only additional adornment. McCandles, I noticed when he arrived, wore a white linen suit, more in keeping with the occasion's demands.

"How the hell can Cantucci afford this?" Sally Archimedes asked me with her usual refinement. She wore a white jump suit that emphasized her powerful build and improbable tan.

"He must spend all his money on these parties." I fetched us both glasses of wine and returned to find McCandles making Sally laugh. Richardson, a black Rhodes Scholar with trendily left-wing views, joined us, and we all talked some more as the band played and a few, stray couples danced. Then came a long clinking of glass—slowly I realized someone was tapping a wine glass with a fork—and Cantucci stood on a chair under the marquee to deliver a toast. Dutifully, we all pushed in under the tent to hear our host.

"It's good to see," he said slowly with wine-induced spittle slightly slurring his speech, "that even this far away from home, we Americans can and *will* make the most of our surroundings and enjoy ourselves. It gives me a lot of pleasure to host this small affair, since being at Oxford, with all the different colleges, means that we don't meet often enough." I detected an Anglicized layer that had coated the Iowa burr of Cantucci's tongue. He was beginning to sound like my college bursar.

"So here we are," he continued, "set down in a strange environment, full of *strange* people," he added, drawing a superior laugh from most of the crowd, "yet able still to come together, as Americans, and with the pride in ourselves and our country that being American inspires."

"Patriotism is the first refuge of a bore," I whispered to Sally Archimedes, but she gave no indication of hearing me. As Cantucci began to speak again I heard McCandles make mock-puking noises. I snorted with laughter until Sally nudged me to be quiet. "I hope," said Cantucci, his voice rising a little, "that in the years ahead when we've all returned home, become established in careers and had families, we will still remember the times we shared in this, our brief period of exile." Exile? "And we'll remember, too, how we never lost sight of our own way of life. The Fourth of July, Thanksgiving, the Kentucky Derby—these are the national holidays we can observe wherever we are. And I myself——"

And he himself what? I wonder to this day. For precisely as Cantucci edged towards self-revelation, he was interrupted by a loud downbeat of a drum and the sudden intrusion of jazz. In the momentary confusion, as attention moved from Cantucci out of the marquee to the now-noisy combo, the tune remained unclear. But soon its piercing notes revealed themselves as the opening bars of "Dixie," played in double time, with double volume. More conspicuous even than this blare was a figure in tails and white tie who stepped jauntily in front of the players and rapidly began a dated vaudevillian dance. It was Andrew Mercy, I saw suddenly, and watched in amazement as his white-gloved hands moved through the air like Al Jolson's. The bizarre timing of this interruption and the sheer weirdness of his dance were less remarkable than Mercy's decision to appear before us in blackface.

The hush that settled on the audience threatened not to break. Finally Sally Archimedes whispered, "Jesus Christ," and Richardson, the black Rhodes Scholar, started to move menacingly towards the dancing figure, his obvious intention to punch in Mercy's shoe polish-covered face. While everyone else maintained an appalled silence, whether from disgust or disbelief, McCandles and I simultaneously (and much to our subsequent disgrace) burst out laughing. It was a long hilarious howl at the absurdity of Mercy, our first lunatic, our first find; and if this joint fit of laughing earned us the opprobrium of our peers, it also sealed our friendship.

Seven

We spent the weekend in London, the first city I can truly say I liked. On Friday night McCandles had dinner with Audrey, and I went to the Connoisseur Club by myself to gamble. I lost fifteen pounds playing blackjack and got drunk at the bar, drinking gin-and-tonics and overtipping the barmaid. She was Polish and kept pumping me for information about jobs in the States. I told her she'd feel at home in Chicago, which is supposed to have more Poles than Warsaw, but since I couldn't provide her with even one name from this legion of countrymen she stopped talking to me and started counting the receipts.

The next day I slept late in the cell-like guest room of Audrey's absent friend, Sarah; then kicked around the Bond Street galleries with McCandles and Audrey. We were asked to leave Agnew's for excessive frivolity. At Audrey's flat in Earl's Court I met her roommate, Celia, and she joined us for dinner at a Kensington bistro. At McCandles' insistence we had three bottles of red wine and then went gambling. I lost another twenty pounds at blackjack by betting stupidly in an effort to impress Celia. She was attractive in a blonde kind of way, with the blotches of flushed red on her arms that occur in my country only through alcoholism. I was drawn to her but felt mildly put off when we ran into what seemed half of the English public school system that evening; she introduced me at various points to Charles, formerly of Stowe, Edward an erstwhile Etonian, and Nicholas, who'd gone to a crammer in Holland Park.

When we left the club it was too late for me to return to Sarah's, so I spent the evening on Audrey's living room floor, next to the daybed that Celia occupied. She and I stayed up late talking, or rather I talked, telling her in very great detail about life in Michigan. At about four in the morning I tried to join her in her bed but was soundly rebuffed. The next day, Sunday, I was badly hung over, a condition which persisted even after two Bloody Marys consumed while reading the papers and ignoring Celia's coolness. I decided to go back to Oxford and said goodbye to Audrey and McCandles. I went down the stairs and out onto the front steps of the row house, where I put down my overnight bag by the dilapidated iron railing and took a bleary look at the square. Derelicts, looking much as I felt, sprawled on benches, while young mothers were forced to stand, ignoring them and keeping a keen eye on their kids. Seedy London, unlike its American counterparts, is rarely threatening; to an outsider, in fact, there is something comical in the prospect of a drunk whipping open his raincoat. With these attractive thoughts stirring slowly in my mind, I reached down for my bag. The front door behind me opened and Celia emerged.

"Hello," I said in embarrassed surprise. "I was just leaving."

"You might have said goodbye." She wore a long coat of dark blue wool with maroon knee-socks and shiny black leather shoes. Her hair was swept back like a lion's mane, a deep gold held in check by a blue band. She was very Sloane for that part of London.

"Are you going back to Oxford?" she asked. I nodded.

"From Paddington?" I nodded again.

"Walking?" I didn't bother to nod, since each affirmative shake of my head sent a mild spasm of nausea shooting downwards through my deteriorating frame.

"Come on," Celia said brusquely, "I'm walking in that direction." I picked up my bag and set off with her, feeling confused by her willingness to accompany me and somewhat embarrassed about my lecherous aggression of the night before. Celia now looked so attractive that I wished I had behaved better, a frequent desire when I am hungover.

We walked north through the dirty streets teeming with the semi-subterranean life of Earl's Court. Celia strode thoroughly oblivious; I, paranoid American, cased every dubious type as it approached.

"Do you work very hard at Oxford?" she asked as we crossed the Cromwell Road. A coach from Victoria ran the light on its way west to Heathrow, and a young girl, obviously American in her lime-green sweater, took our photograph from its back seat as it passed.

"Not really, though I'm supposed to now. I've got my exams this term."

"Have you enjoyed it there?"

"Yes," I said, nodding gently. The air was doing me good.

"Lucky you," she said deeply. When I said nothing she added, "I would like to have gone to Oxford. But I was too thick." This was said without self-deprecation.

"You don't seem very stupid to me," I said with a laugh. The candor of the English is refreshing, and best taken head-on. At first, it's a little shocking to hear an English parent say one of his children is smarter than another, to watch them call a spastic just that. But the surprise wears off quickly, and it is the American gift for euphemism that starts to annoy.

"Did you go to university?" I asked.

"For a while. I was at University College London for six months but I couldn't bear it. I'm an art historian," she said, then corrected herself, "or at least I'd like to be one."

"What period are you interested in?" I asked, imagining her writing a thesis about her relatives' Georgian houses.

"Victorian architecture," she said curtly. "Gothic in the 19th century. And follies—I like follies. But actually right now I can only call it my hobby; it's not a living. I want to go to the Courtauld as soon as I have the money."

Sure, I thought sardonically, you mean as soon as papa comes up with the cash. When people ask me how the English manage, with a cost of living equal to New York's and half the salary, I either say "not very well" or "independent means." What I'd give for independent means, I thought then with an unflattering tinge of self-pity, forgetting that my grandfather had left me some money. My parents had plenty of money but they pushed all their children out of the house when we turned twenty-one, with lots of encouragement and a firm kick in the ass. It is not an attitude I fully under-stood, and, no, I was not grateful for the lessons this artificial self-sufficiency was commonly supposed to have taught me. All it ever really did was make me envy the trust funds of my wealthy fellows in boarding school and university. Bro-kers, securities analysts, "a little man I have to see down-town"—how I begrudged them the minor inconveniences of inherited money.

Something of my jealousy must now have shown when, with a patronizing sigh, I said, "I suppose your parents will help you out."

We had turned into Kensington High Street and when Celia stopped short we were directly across from the gates to Holland Park. I turned around to find her looking at me sharply. "What do you mean?" she asked. "Whatever makes you think my parents could help me out?"

Still enchanted with British candor, I said sarcastically, "You don't strike me as a product of poverty. I shouldn't think your father welded doors on a British Leyland assembly line."

"That's not the point." She stepped closer to me and I realized she was very annoyed. "You take a lot for granted," she said harshly, pointing a finger at my chest. "Why do you make all these easy assumptions? How are you to know who my parents are or what sort of class I'm from? It's not very American of you, is it?" she added with her own sarcasm, less snide than mine. "I thought you were all supposed to be so democratic."

"A thousand apologies ma'am," I said, a little like Jimmy Stewart in midwestern abjection before Katherine Hepburn. But Celia was unpacified by this.

"Just what are you playing at? Here you go talking to me as if I were Princess Anne, but last night you seemed to think an evening's polite conversation entitled you to a quick leg-over. What was *that* about, may I ask?"

I shrugged again, not a very assertive response. "You can't blame me for trying. I don't believe it was entirely unexpected."

"It was," she said decisively. "I don't mind the odd advance—it's quite flattering when one's ready for it—but not on that short notice. You probably think it was merely cheeky—a bit of daring that didn't come off."

"I wouldn't say that."

"What exactly would you say? You don't seem to mind one way or the other."

This wasn't true at all but I despaired of making that clear. I don't know what it is—some form of social retardation, I guess—but I project an air of profound indifference precisely when I am most upset. True to form, I now threw up my hands in a gesture of, well, profound indifference.

"Is that all you can say?" She, too, threw her hands up in mimicry. "Christ, you really are something, aren't you?" She started to walk away, back down the High Street, and it was this move that must have precipitated my action. I took three quick steps and moved around to face her. She stopped and looked at me, furious. "I'm sorry," I said with some urgency. "I'm really sorry. It's just that I'm not any good at saying I'm sorry." She said nothing and I continued. "Couldn't we start all over again? Forget about last night and pretend we've just met? You know, make a fresh start of knowing each other."

"A fresh start," she said shortly. "You want a fresh start."

"Yes, exactly. Come have lunch with me in Oxford sometime, or let me take you to tea here in London. It'll be completely aboveboard, I promise."

"Tea at the Tate," she said with a sudden laugh. "That would be nice. But I can't. I'll be working."

"What, on your architectural work? Can't you take an afternoon off? Or see me on a weekend?"

"No, it's not that," she said, shaking her head. "I'll be on a tour—I'm a tour guide, that's what lets me pay the rent. I show groups of Japs around the countryside. Welcome to beautiful Woburn Abbey. Here is the historic Longleat. Et-cetera, et-cetera," she said rather like Yul Brynner in *The King and I*.

"God, how awful."

"Don't start that again," she said crossly. "It's not awful at all. I like the Japs, they're very polite. They tip me very well and they never make passes. Unlike some people I know."

"Well, when can I see you then?"

She looked mildly amused. "I'll be gone for over a month. And besides, aren't you going to be busy? Haven't you got your exams soon?"

I dismissed them with an airy wave of the hand. "They don't matter."

"Really? I'd have thought they mattered very much."

I then had a mild inspiration. "Look, why don't you come meet me when I get out of Schools? McCandles and Audrey should be there, you could drive up with her."

Celia looked thoughtful for a moment. "Come on," I pleaded, "It'll be fun. I promise."

"I'll see what I can do," she said with a slow smile, then looked at her watch. "I'd better be going. I hadn't meant to walk this far. Good luck on your exams."

I wanted to part company with some show of warmth and a sudden surplus of affection moved me to lean over and kiss her goodbye. With my eyes half-closed it took a moment to realize that I was kissing the air, though it was air that smelled faintly of Celia's mild perfume. I opened my eyes to find her two steps away and looking at me cynically.

"Do grow up," she said quietly and turned on her heel. I watched as she moved down the street, walking with firm, independent strides, then took myself in far less confident fashion through Hyde Park towards Paddington.

Eight

I caught the train and was back in college in time for dinner. After gray lamb and treacle tart, I drank some port out of a water glass and read the early Auden until I fell asleep with my pants on and one shoe off.

I awoke to a loud and terrifying explosion. For a moment, caught in a web of sleep, I was still in the world of Auden:

> O it's broken the lock and splintered the door
> O it's the gate where they're turning, turning;
> Their boots are heavy on the floor
> and their eyes are burning.

Fortunately, the lock held firm until I regained my senses and opened the door.

It was Bicker.

"Hey!" he shouted.

"Bicker," I said with as much enthusiasm as I could muster.

He strode past me into the room, which now seemed more miniature than ever since he towered over the furniture. As he sat down, his long frame seemed to consume the chair.

"How are you?" he asked briskly. "Aren't you happy to see me?"

"Charlie," I said getting him a water glass and filling it with port, "I'm always glad to see you. It's just that I was sleeping."

"Sorry," he said, totally unapologetic. "So what's going on?"

"The usual. When did you get back?"

"This morning. I've been looking for you and McCandles all day. Where is he?"

"In London with Audrey. He should be back by now. Did you bring any cigarettes?" Bicker always brought back duty-free cigarettes for McCandles and me.

"Yeh. I got you each two cartons. They didn't have your brand though—"

"They didn't have Winstons?"

"I thought you smoked Pall Malls. Anyway, I got you two cartons of Salems."

"Jesus Christ," I said softly and poured myself some port.

"What's the matter?"

"Nothing. So how was the legislature?"

"Great. Listen, you have to come up next time you're back. Your uncle keeps asking about you." The uncle he referred to was a New Hampshire state senator; Bicker was a state representative. Although politically opposed, they had established a small relationship in my honor.

"Maybe I will in the summer," I said.

"Are you coming to my talk?"

"When is it?"

"Tuesday. It's on PACs."

"Packs of Salems?"

Bicker didn't laugh. He could be charmingly ambivalent about his own successes, but, however mixed his feelings, they did not include self-deprecation. He said, "Political Action Committees."

"Did Stoneface pick the topic?"

"No. I did. It's an interesting topic. You have to come, okay?"

"Okay," I said. I was fully awake now and went to the basin and threw water on my face to confirm it. "Let's go see if McCandles is back yet. And I want to hear all about your legislative triumphs."

Charlie Bicker was tall and brash and the most successful person I had ever met. He was not yet twenty-five but already in his second term in the New Hampshire state legislature. That body met for eleven hectic weeks in late winter and early spring, so Bicker would leave Oxford in late January and return in late April. This caused havoc with his tutorial schedule and extended his stay at Oxford by a year, but Bicker handled the resulting uncertainty, as he managed all mundane difficulties, with unflappable ease.

He had graduated from Princeton *summa cum laude* and reached Oxford on a Rhodes Scholarship. He had founded a successful newspaper in his New Hampshire hometown and in addition to his legislative duties worked as a peripatetic adviser to one of New Hampshire's United States senators. He was, to boot, attractive to women; a tall lanky figure with an unruly mop of straw-colored hair and razor features that really did recall the young Abe Lincoln. Bicker, in short, had everything going for him.

McCandles and I liked him just the same. His self-assurance was accompanied by true modesty as well, and a willingness (rare in a Rhodes Scholar) to play second fiddle to a louder or more interesting set of strings. And Bicker's brashness brought with it a refreshing honesty that McCandles and I, professional dissemblers and essentially misanthropic, admired without reservation. The Rhodes Scholars then at Oxford all seemed to want to be senators, and they acted accordingly in the manner they thought necessary for that role.

Some were quite brilliant; some were astonishingly dull; all were accomplished in the dubious art of impressing their seniors and filling their peers with envious awe. They were always so tactful, bringing to the simplest act of friendship a diplomatic subtlety that I thought had expired with Dean Acheson. They remembered names, nicknames, alma maters, hometowns, birthdays and, less openly, other peoples' failures; and they would greet the most casual acquaintance—encountered in Cornmarket, seen at the gym—with the oiliness politicians exude as they turn from their chicken and peas to pump hands with their fund-raising dinnermates.

In contrast, Bicker *was* a politician; he had fought campaigns, sat on committees, sponsored legislation. Yet instead of the greased palm, the solicitous inquiry into your Aunt Minnie's health, Bicker was candid to the point of awkwardness, blunt verging on boorish. "What do *you* want?" he would sneer at glad-handing acquaintances he considered too distant for such familiarity; "You're completely wrong!" he would snap at fellow Rhodes Scholars as they pontificated with Republican ease on SALT, the Congressional elections, or the Connecticut blue laws. Bicker operated on the teenage principle of calling an asshole an asshole, and although one day he might become Governor of New Hampshire, he would never be elected secretary of his year of Rhodes Scholars.

Next to McCandles, Bicker was my closest friend at Oxford, and the three of us formed a tight trio of friendship. We represented a curious mix: Bicker, faithful to his friends but scornful, at least initially, of all strangers; McCandles openly cynical of everyone and everything; and myself, still uncertain, to be honest, about the essential nature of my species.

The "Terrible Troika," Audrey called us, and I suppose there was a fierceness to our amity that repelled outside acquaintances. We drank heavily together and indulged in the kind of horseplay that boarding school is supposed to exhaust. We could be found, even on weekday evenings, careening through the quads of our respective colleges with an unmistakable air of aggressive revelry. We simply did not take Oxford seriously, an attitude quite common among the English undergraduates, who were late to shed their adolescence, but rare among American students, who were respectful of the place and career bound.

Not that we three would be careerless or were immune to the missionary ambition that afflicts my generation, the somber successors to the Sixties. But each of us—McCandles, Bicker, and I—saw Oxford as a charmed interval in our lives, an adjournment, as it were, from the long trial to come. Of us three, clearly Bicker had the brightest future lying ahead of him, and this made his abdication from sobriety and self-advancement while at Oxford all the more remarkable. Not all traces of ambition were shed, since for Bicker anonymity was an unknown condition. Just as in America he knew journalists and politicians from midtown Manhattan to Georgetown, so too in England he cultivated acquaintance among the notables. Nor did he rely on chance meetings to forge these relations with the great; instead, he wrote frank letters of self-introduction, then let his credentials do the rest. Usually it worked; he spent an afternoon with Harold Wilson on the basis of his Rhodes Scholarship. And when it didn't, Bicker moved on to his next target, unperturbed. His coming talk on PACs, moreover, was just one in a series he had given over the course of his three years at Oxford.

The night of the "Terrible Troika's" reunion we began in McCandles' rooms, drinking gin and orange juice while Bicker told us tales of his legislative winter. McCandles pressed him for news about the States that would never make the pages of the *International Herald Tribune*. We also heard details of Bicker's bills, passed or shot down, and we counseled him in *post facto* fashion, elevating those issues that dimly touched the lives of his eight thousand constituents to the status of international concern. Abroad, one's worries about home are inevitably magnified by the inflating effects of distance, but Bicker brought us down to earth; he disappointed our dramatic expectations of mass recession and breadlines in America. We reciprocated by pooh-poohing the prospects of the Labour Party's ascension to power and by deflating the exaggerated American vision of the left-wing Tony Benn's importance. Bicker had once spent two hours with Benn on a London-to-Manchester train and ever since had been insufferably optimistic about the MP's chances of becoming Britain's Lenin.

When we had drunk all of McCandles' gin, we walked down to Magdalen, Bicker's college, to drink beer in the common room. Spring was in sufficient gear to mark the evening; mixed with the soot and bus exhaust in the High Street came the sweet moist smell of flower boxes and turf. Our conversation turned to Oxford, and it was interesting to watch Bicker's enthusiasm, which had not had time to flag to the levels of McCandles' cynicism.

"Nothing has happened," McCandles declared as we walked past Queen's College. "Nothing at all."

"That's not true," I said, fearing McCandles talking about boredom would dampen our mood. "There's always Newcastle."

"Oh that," McCandles said and waved his hand in irritation.

"What happened?" asked Bicker. He knew Newcastle about as well as I did, which meant slightly, but ideologically he shared many of Newcastle's left-wing assumptions.

"Nothing happened," McCandles said stubbornly.

"Tell him," I said. "Go on, he'll be interested."

"Yes, tell me," Bicker said eagerly. "I want to know."

And so, over pints of lager in the Magdalen Graduate Common Room (deserted at that hour, it was after midnight), McCandles told Bicker about Newcastle's obsession with Lafayette Jackson. Bicker was a good listener for a politician and stayed silent throughout McCandles' recitation; McCandles wrongly took his silence for lack of interest. "I told you it was nothing," he concluded defensively.

"What do you mean?" Bicker said excitedly. "It's terrific. Don't you know about this Jackson woman?"

McCandles and I turned to each other in bafflement. "What do you mean?" we said almost simultaneously.

"She's a *pig*," Bicker said sternly, as if he were a priest describing a heretic, or a Moslem rejecting an invitation to a barbecue. "She's a neoconservative pig. She's on that ridiculous committee about the present danger."

"Really?" I asked in wonder. I can't say I was surprised by the nature of her politics as much as by the fact that she had politics at all. My image of her centered around an anonymous Vietnamese orphan, hardly a politicized vision.

"Absolutely," Bicker declared confidently.

"I didn't know she had any political interests," McCandles said, as if reading my thoughts.

"It's probably recent," Bicker said, speaking of it as though she had just acquired a lymphoma.

"But she writes for the *New York Review*," I protested.

"It doesn't matter. She's a right-winger, believe me. Especially in her field."

"Southern history?" I asked.

"Yes," Bicker said emphatically. He had majored in history at Princeton.

"Is that true?" I asked McCandles.

"I suppose so," he said wearily, and I took this to mean he didn't know for sure. He looked bored and suddenly sang out in the exaggerated *basso profundo* of Preservation Hall: "I'se happy to be a slave/Serve de Massa to my grave."

"Is that what she says?" I asked Bicker.

"Something like that," said Bicker. "Right-wing revisionism."

I cannot say this news troubled me as much as Bicker clearly thought it should. Half my family finds its politics somewhere to the right of Mussolini, and if I let ideology prevail in such relationships I would be practically an orphan. Bicker, on the other hand, was perfectly happy to judge people by their political opinions.

"Anyway, I thought her book was about some island. With a slave community," I said.

"Some mythical island," said McCandles sourly.

"Her portrayal of it's pretty mythical," Bicker said harshly. " 'All them nigras happy as Tom Sawyer floating on the raft'."

"Actually, it was Huck Finn," I said.

"Well, you know what I mean," said Bicker, but I wasn't sure I did. His neofascist Lafayette Jackson was not the woman I had encountered.

"Let's go ride the deer," McCandles said suddenly. I realized then how much we'd been drinking.

"Count me out," I said and stood up to leave. "I've got to get some sleep. I've got Schools in five weeks."

"Oh, come on," scoffed McCandles. "You've got lots of time left to study. Let's go ride Bambi."

"You two go. I can't keep my eyes open." This would be the only acceptable excuse to my companions, but actually I have hunted deer since I was nine years old and I find the captive miniatures of Magdalen simply revolting. Somehow attempting to ride one seemed the ultimate degradation, for both rider and deer. I walked out with my two friends, side-stepping McCandles as he tried half-playfully to push me into the Old Quad. Drink always made him physically

aggressive. We parted ways by the chapel, with Bicker shout-
ing across the sward that I must come to his talk in Nuffield.
I nodded a weary assent and walked slowly up the darkened
High Street, to college and to bed.

Nine

Bicker was an impressive public speaker—forthright, articulate, even charming when addressing small groups. I had seen him on the stump and in the classroom; in both settings, he was masterful.

In Nuffield College the Wednesday after our reunion, he spoke in an oversized classroom on the ground floor. As usual, Willoughby presided. Although Hubert was the doyen of American studies in Oxford, Willoughby was another eminence, leaving to Hubert the staider historical areas of Civil War studies and the 1890s (about which, despite Newcastle's 1943 line of demarcation, Hubert really did know something), garnering for himself all claim to current domestic politics. Willoughby knew a tremendous amount about American political life, and he specialized in arcana about the men and methods of old-fashioned political machines. He knew Mayor Daley's widow's maiden name and the exact number of stiffs who voted for JFK in the tainted election of 1960; he had personal acquaintance with Meade Esposito and could tell you how many New York state assemblymen were born in Brooklyn. He could tell you, and he did; possibly his recitations would have interested the denizens of Chicago's Bridgeport or of Brooklyn Heights, but I found them boring beyond belief.

In fact, only the comedy of Willoughby's appearance lent interest to any encounter with him. We called him "Stone-face," a deliberate misnomer since there was always some expression at work on his features. His facial contours were difficult to distinguish since they moved in loose disjunction whenever he was talking, which was most of the time. Tufts of whiskers the size of an old threepenny bit popped up in odd crannies on odd days; McCandles once told Bicker that Willoughby shaved with a spoon. Unlike Hubert, his sternly fastidious colleague, Willoughby brought a persistent sloppiness to all his activities—talking or teaching (indistinguishable to him), or even eating, which he did chiefly with his fingers since he held an unusual affection for the deep-fried fast food ubiquitous in America and rapidly securing a foothold in Britain.

That night Willoughby introduced Bicker to the audience in a lengthy panegyric that embarrassed even McCandles and me, Bicker's supporters and friends. What prompted his out-burst of admiration was unclear, although I'm sure it had more than a little to do with Bicker's real, if comparatively minor, status as an elected public official. In the manner of Hubert, Willoughby doubtless saw Bicker in the line of Ful-bright, Bradley and Clinton, and looked forward to the day when he could say, "When he was my student, Senator Bicker said to me. . . . " Willoughby had rather less to say for the run-of-the-mill undergraduate.

The crowd was large for a Wednesday evening spent in the dreary confines of Nuffield. The psephologists were out in force, eager to talk votes. They were named for the Greek word for ballot, which was a pebble—or *psephus*. A don in my own college had coined this term for the statistical students of elections and voting, but now aspirations to this political science version of bean-counting entailed a life sentence in Nuffield College.

The historians, too, were present in number, at least those with an American interest to parade. Hubert waddled in, Gladstone bag on one arm, Lafayette Jackson on the other, and the two joined Sutro in seats near the door. I sat with McCandles and Audrey, who was up for a mid-week visit. As the show began, I noticed Newcastle slink in furtively and sit directly behind Hubert and Lafayette Jackson. I had not seen him since our tea in the Science Building.

Bicker's talk was short and not too dull—if you were interested in PACs. I had downed a large whiskey in my room before attending so I felt no pain as the electoral interests of corporations were outlined in the passionate voice of the progressive New Hampshire legislator. I suppressed a laugh as the image of another Bicker entered my head—drunk and loud in a Magdalen quad. When Bicker finished, Stoneface stood up and asked for questions. The first two were innocuous and easily handled by Bicker. Then the stronger stuff emerged.

"I fail to understand the logic you employ in reaching your conclusion." The speaker was Hubert, his voice gaining a barrister's resonance as he continued. "You suggest in some detail—though I am not entirely convinced—that PACs are largely tools of corporate enterprise in America. How, from this argument, you decide that electoral politics is thus a corrupt form of corporate gamesmanship I quite fail to see." He paused, then added with an uncordial twist, "Perhaps you could enlighten me?"

McCandles looked at me with a mixture of trepidation and amusement at our friend's interrogation; we watched to see how Bicker would cope. "Simple," said Bicker, entirely unfazed. "PACs have become a crucial element in the funding of campaigns, and they allow corporations to funnel large sums of money to the candidates of their choice. The new limits on corporate donations are meaningless. You now have cases where twenty executives of a corporation give the limit to some Republican candidate and allow him to outspend and outadvertise his opponent."

Hubert replied, "Surely you're not suggesting that inequities in campaign expenditure are something new."

Another voice interrupted before Bicker could respond. "Historical precedent doesn't justify contemporary wrongs."

It was Newcastle, speaking from behind Hubert who ignored the remark and looked to Bicker for an answer. But Bicker merely nodded at what Newcastle said, until the tension of the exchange was relieved by one of the psephologists, who asked a question about voting patterns that not even the Great Vote Counter in the sky could have answered.

Then a black girl with an upper-class English accent asked a question and the subject moved to foreign policy, as it always does when you discuss American politics in a foreign environment. Soon Bicker was declaiming a litany of American errors, especially those concerning Central America, then much in the news. An unfortunate topic, really, for Bicker to expound upon, since he didn't know a banana republic from the Falkland Islands. It was a case of enthusiasm winning out over prudence; similarly, Bicker had during the last year been proclaiming his desire to visit Cuba. Such radical enthusiasms were not uncommon for him, but by embracing them so noisily, Bicker sometimes made me fear for his political future. On the whole, however, they were exhibited only in Oxford, and I had come to realize that the New Hampshire voters were spared the more extreme of his passing ideological fancies.

But in Nuffield College Bicker felt free to cut loose. What the political columnist would call a harsh torrent of invective poured forth as Bicker recounted American follies and failures in the countries adjoining Mexico's lower half. "Like Vietnam," "excessive anticommunism," "repressive dictatorships"—the phrases tumbled out like an especially bad article in the *Nation*. McCandles rolled his eyes; across the room, Newcastle nodded vigorously with each fresh assertion.

When Lafayette Jackson stood up, the lights in the room flickered for a moment and there was an undergraduate snicker or two at the apparent causality. She looked flustered and asked her question in a quiet voice.

"I can't hear you," said Bicker in his inimitable fashion that straddled the line between candor and rudeness.

"Let me repeat my question." The voice was still soft. "Is there really any evidence that our government could profitably side with the insurgents?"

"We could at least be neutral," said Bicker. I think they were talking about Nicaragua.

"If the Soviets pick a side, doesn't that to some extent dictate what side we end up on?"

"My point is exactly that we shouldn't let what the Soviets do determine our own policy. It's that kind of reflex that gets us into trouble."

"Historically, when we've stayed out of this kind of situation our interests have suffered."

Bicker shook his head. "Not our interests—the United Fruit Company's interests."

Newcastle again entered the exchange. "There is a distinction, you know."

This was open rudeness, and Lafayette Jackson turned around in surprise. She was clearly unused to the give-and-take that characterized question periods at Oxford. "I know that," she said, sounding aggrieved in her meek way.

"It wasn't clear in your article," Newcastle said snidely.

Her piece must have appeared, and she now looked embarrassed, saying timidly, "I think my article recognized the distinction."

"Not at all," Newcastle said crisply. "It founders on this very point."

"Well," said Lafayette Jackson hesitantly, "perhaps we can

discuss that some other time." She turned back to Bicker but not before Newcastle delivered a parting shot. "I plan to," he said ominously.

This mini–dialogue had derailed any larger discussion; there were no more questions and the meeting broke up. Newcastle was quick to leave, and I saw Hubert and Lafayette Jackson walk out together, talking with Sutro. I hung around, waiting with McCandles and Audrey for Bicker, who was under seige by the psephologists. At last he detached himself, and the four of us walked through a light drizzle to the Nag's Head for a drink. To McCandles' delight, a drunk was leaning over the canal bridge, vomiting with loud moans into the water below. "Picturesque Oxford!" McCandles cried out, like a seller of postcards, until Audrey made him be quiet. Suddenly from behind us came a light, trotting sound of feet. It was Newcastle, carrying an overnight bag, or rather a vinyl athletic bag with *Adidas* boldly illuminated on its side. It must be borrowed, I thought, for Newcastle was entirely unathletic. He was whistling loudly, though jerkily as he was running, and McCandles later claimed the tune was recognizably the "Internationale."

"I'm off to London," Newcastle explained, slowing down for a moment as he passed.

"To see your mother?" I asked somewhat maliciously, remembering how he hated her.

"Of course not," he said tersely. "I've got books due at the British Library. I'll be there first thing," he said, as if to remove any doubt from our minds that this was a *business* trip.

"Good," said Bicker. "Work hard." This with the slight sarcasm it took a close friend to detect.

Newcastle did not discern it, saying, "Yes. Quite. Anyway, well done, Charles. We showed her tonight."

Bicker looked mildly taken aback, for he was not used to authoritative praise from his peers who either, as friends, joshed him or, as enemies, found points to criticize.

"Have a good time," said Audrey incongruously, as Newcastle resumed his jog towards the train. McCandles laughed at this. We continued towards the pub as the figure of Newcastle receded down the street.

"It was a good talk," I said to Bicker.

"Thanks. I thought the questions were pretty weird."

"Professor Hubert had a lot to say," McCandles remarked.

"What's his problem?" asked Bicker. "Is he some kind of pluralist who thinks every interest should have its own PAC?"

"Who knows?" said McCandles as we entered the pub, adding mischievously, "he probably just doesn't like you."

"Well, I don't like him. And that Jackson woman is a real pain in the ass," said Bicker, loud enough to turn the heads of the bar regulars.

"Is that what Newcastle was talking about?" I asked.

"I saw him this afternoon," McCandles interrupted, "and he told me Lafayette Jackson's article had appeared. It was all he could talk about—that, and the letter he's going to write attacking it."

"If her article's anything like her reactionary questions tonight," said Bicker irritatedly, "Newcastle *ought* to attack it. You should encourage him."

"No," I said, spooning two ice cubes into my drink, thinking how aggressive and hostile Newcastle had been to Lafayette Jackson. It was like the guerrilla attacks of American students on "authority" in the 1960s; the essential courtesy of public discourse at a place like Oxford made it seem very harsh indeed.

"Why not?"

I started to answer fairly heatedly when McCandles intervened. "You're missing the point," he said gently to Bicker. "Newcastle doesn't need any more encouragement. The boy's obsessed."

Ten

I began studying hard for my final exams, panicked by the thought of receiving Third Class Honours. The exams were called Schools, after the T. G. Jackson building in which they were taken. I would have eight exams in all, each lasting three hours and requiring answers to four questions. One could receive "Honours" in three classes: First (even rarer than *summa cum laude* in the States); Second, a catch-all for the bright but lazy, or hardworking but average; or Third, for the lazy *and* dumb. Although an American senator once boasted in his campaign literature of having received "Third highest honors" at Oxford, a Third was in fact very bad news. It was this disaster I now sought to avoid. Bill Bradley got a Third; so did Auden; but I wasn't tall enough to play basketball and my poems were metrically unsound.

So I buckled down to my schoolwork, trying to generate an interest in the doctrines of Anscombe and Geach. I was working weekends now, more from fear than diligence, and I declined McCandles' offer to go to London. Bicker joined him there on Saturday, so I found myself alone, bad-tempered, and working while the rest of Oxford played. I thought of seeing Celia and phoned her, but Audrey answered and I pretended to be looking for McCandles. I casually mentioned Celia, and Audrey said she was in Bath with two coachloads of Japanese.

I had dinner by myself Saturday night in an Indian restaurant in the Turl, then stopped in the graduate common room before resuming work. My college, as I've said before, is an intimate, fairly informal place, at least compared with the rituals and intricate social stratifications of Christ Church or Magdalen. The Fellows of my college, for example, occasionally visited our common room, a mingling of social ranks unheard of elsewhere in the university. So I was not surprised that Saturday night to find two dons there, talking with Krattenstein. I was somewhat taken aback to find Lafayette Jackson with them.

"Come join us," said Krattenstein amiably, so I drew up a chair and said hello to the others. Both dons nodded to me civilly and Lafayette smiled, which suggested that she remembered me. She was conspicuously dressed up, much like my grandmother in Michigan at Sunday lunch in a fancy restaurant, although Lafayette lacked the raccoon coat to fill out the parallel. She wore a formal suit of grey wool, a modest string of graduated pearls, and sling-backed low-heeled pumps. Her posture was equally formal; one of the dons slouched in a pose of post-prandial relaxation—legs crossed, arms dangled down the sides of his chair—but Lafayette sat upright like a convent girl waiting to see Mother Superior.

"We've just been to dinner," the don named Lidodes announced and I wanted to say "No!" in feigned disbelief. He continued grandly, "And a very good dinner it was, if I say so myself."

I should describe Lidodes—a history don whom snottier students nicknamed "Chiasmus"—if only because he was one of the few members of college I actively disliked. He was commonly called a don of the old school, which as far as I could tell meant only that he was pompous and anti-American. Despite his surname, he was English and had taken a Double First at Cambridge. A great barrel of a man, with dark features and a five o'clock shadow that appeared by lunch, Lidodes exuded a self-confidence that was aggressive and hearty. He could almost be described as clubbable, but his was a nasty *bonhommie* since his small talk consisted of strings of "witty" remarks, made invariably at the expense of others, usually his dimmer students. He spoke, moreover, with a kind of gross, inflated pedantry I usually associate with the ill-educated trying to look clever. Lidodes would have got a Third from Fowler.

If I found Lidodes unusually self-satisfied, he certainly didn't show much pleasure at the sight of me. And his disdain, which seemed to have originated with my nationality, was compounded, doubtless with some justice, by my known aversion to serious academic work. In his eyes I was a dilettante; he was a creep in mine; for each of us every feature of the other was a source of irritation. I found his incongruities of dress, for example, more annoying than I would in a foppish friend, and tonight I found him ridiculous; he wore evening dress when Krattenstein and Hall, the other don, were content with suits.

Lafayette turned towards Lidodes and said warmly, "Howard just loves Italian food. It was a real treat for us both." I must have looked curious about "Howard," for Krattenstein said "Mr. Jackson" informatively.

"Ah," I said and looked at Lafayette Jackson. "Your husband."

"Yes," she said. I noticed that she kept her hands clasped ceremoniously in her lap and sat with both feet flat on the floor, as if obeying the parietal rules of a Southern sorority—"when entertaining male visitors, or being entertained by them, girls are reminded to keep the door ajar and their feet firmly on the floor." The unease I'd sensed at the History Faculty party seemed even greater here. Lafayette broke my reverie by adding, "He should be back in a minute. He's just gone for cigarettes." This drew Howard to my bosom since Lidodes was known to be pathologically anti-smoking.

"After so many High Table dinners," Lafayette said to Lidodes, "I'm surprised to find such a good restaurant in Oxford." She suddenly blushed, perhaps realizing that this remark might be thought rude. She said quickly, "After all, why go out when you have such delectable food in Hall?" Why indeed, I thought cynically, envisaging the stuff we lower orders regularly consumed at "Low Table"—within sight of the upper echelon yet culinary light years away.

"One likes a change from time to time," said Lidodes grandly, and this provoked me to speak up. I am not argumentative *per se*—it is not a character trait as far as I can tell—but if Jesus Himself got on my nerves I would be tempted to ask Him just who His father was.

"Actually, there's a large non-academic side to Oxford," I said to Lafayette and added, "a very prosperous side, too. There's a lot of industry here." Lidodes looked at me as if I had broken wind in the Queen Mother's presence. So I continued, "Have you seen the car works? British Leyland has a large plant just out of town on the ring road."

"Not yet," said Lafayette gaily. "But I'll add it to the list. I've told Howard, I won't go home until I've seen everything I've made a note of."

"I shouldn't bother with the Cowley works," said Lidodes, and Hall nodded unctuously next to him. "I'm afraid you would find them vastly inferior to your own Detroit."

"Different," I said emphatically, wondering what acquaintance Lafayette might have with the Motor City. I added, "But you won't hear much about Cowley here in the university. The town–gown split is enormous."

"It is in Maryland, too," said Lafayette. "And yet I think it's so important to be aware of the local community, to be conscious of their goals."

"Really?" inquired Lidodes skeptically. "Then I'm very much afraid that I'm in need of what seems to be referred to as 'consciousness raising.'"

Lafayette blushed slightly. "Well actually," she said appeasingly, "I can't pretend that the two communities have much in common."

"Nothing save mutual loathing," said Lidodes. "'Should the town raise up its head, draw your sword and lay it dead'," he declaimed, leaving me guessing as to the quotation's provenance. Betjeman's brother? Tennyson's wife? Hall laughed loudly at the lines and Lafayette smiled, slightly puzzled. She struck me as capable of agreeing with anything; if I had disliked her I could have compounded her unease simply by disagreeing with everything Lidodes said, forcing her to shuttle back and forth like a marionette between his and my diametrically opposed opinions.

As I resisted the temptation to expand perversely upon the beauties of the Cowley works, the door to the common room was suddenly flung open. It was a door with a habit of sticking; when it would at last give way, it tended to do so with startling speed and even more startling results. Now a middle-aged man in a brown suit swung with the door. Only by suddenly releasing the doorknob did he manage to avoid smacking into the common room wall. This was a big man, and his size was emphasized by his lurching, momentary imbalance, and by the surge of his shoulders as he caught himself and jerked his frame upright to an erect position. The surprise in his face and a wet glaze to his lips struck me as indisputable evidence that he was tight as a drum.

"Howard," Lafayette exclaimed.

"Honey," said Howard with the fond embarrassment of a man caught peeing in his own backyard.

There was a sticky pause for a moment which Krattenstein dispelled by jumping to his feet. "Can I get you something to drink, Mr. Jackson?" he asked, as if the man might otherwise go thirsty through intellectual absorption in the biography of Carrie Nation. "We have lager or bitter," Krattenstein added a little mischievously, since he himself was drinking coffee.

Eagerness spread like soft butter across Howard Jackson's face. "Anything," he said enthusiastically, and Krattenstein poured him a full pint of lager. Howard Jackson came and sat next to me; Krattenstein joined us, making introductions.

When he heard my voice Howard's face lit up. "You're American, too. It's good to hear our mother tongue again."

Lidodes winced at this and kept talking to Lafayette Jackson. "How do you like it here?" Howard asked me.

"Just fine. How about you?"

"Swell," he said loudly, looking over at his wife. Then he moved his boozy face close to my shoulder and said more quietly, "But I'll be glad to get home."

"I'll bet," I said affably.

"Don't get me wrong, I'm sure it's swell being a student here. But I'm no scholar," he said, a less surprising self-assessment than perhaps he realized.

"But you like books, don't you? Your wife was telling me about the booksellers you've been seeing."

He smiled a little. "Sure, I like books." He paused. "They're a business, of course. Just like anything else."

"A commodity?" I suggested.

"*Exactimento!*" He drank some more beer. "You can buy them or sell them just like baked beans. Not that many people would see it that way around here."

"Do you collect them?"

"I'd prefer to say I invest in them. Manuscripts mainly, autographs, letters—that sort of historical material. It's through my wife's work that I've gotten a little bit involved. I make the odd play here and there."

"What do you think of the British market then?"

"For books? Kind of slow. And snooty. There's one guy in London I kind of like named Sam Goodiston. A real businessman. A funny little Jewish fellow but I like him."

I thought Krattenstein would swallow his beer mug; I can't say I was wild about the formulation, either. "Have another beer, Mr. Jackson," I said, not without sarcasm.

"Sure thing," he said, like a fat man on his second pass through the smorgasbord. But just as Howard started to hand me his glass, his wife interrupted. "That's kind of you," she announced, picking her purse up from the floor, "but I think we should be going. We've had such a lovely time tonight that we wouldn't want to spoil it by overstaying our welcome."

Lidodes and Hall made perfunctory protest but Lafayette ignored them and looked at Howard. He stared back at her, loosening his nylon tie with a big hand, but his eyes were soft and compliant. He looked cowed, almost sad, and he made me think of a midwestern barber in a Ring Lardner story, keen to please, amoral and spineless, intent only on being one of the boys. The barber in my fantasy talked to his wife on an old-fashioned telephone, leaning forward to speak in the black mouthpiece while his cronies played pinochle in the back room. "Yes Amelia," the barber said in low tones of resignation, "I'll be home to supper right away." So, too, Howard nodded slowly at his wife. "Okay, honey. Whatever you say." And he and Lafayette made their farewells and said their thanks.

After they had left, Hall immediately began speaking to Lidodes. I looked at Krattenstein who rolled his eyes slowly heavenward, not in distaste but wonder. "A chore?" I said slowly. He shrugged his shoulders. "Fun?" I said, more skeptically. He put both palms out like a less zany Zero Mostel.

"I wouldn't go that far," he said. "Nice people, but hardly fun."

"The husband seems pretty good value. I liked the bit about a funny little Jewish fellow whom he liked nonetheless."

Krattenstein raised his eyebrows and then looked serious. "He's all right, I guess. If you're interested in money." You would never have guessed that Krattenstein's father owned dress shops in Montreal.

I stood up and got myself a pint of lager. When I returned Lidodes turned his attention to me. I sensed that my earlier remarks infused his opening comment with a certain acid bite. "So how are you getting on?" he asked, aware of my approaching Finals.

I shrugged my shoulders and resisted the temptation to talk about my exams. Nothing the History don told me would make a difference to my results.

"It doesn't really matter, does it, how you do?" asked Krattenstein.

"You're not going to law school?" said Hall.

I shook my head. Hall asked with concern, "What about graduate school? Won't you be a graduate student?"

"Never," I said decisively.

"Why not?" asked Hall innocently, and it was my turn to ask him a question.

"Have you ever met an American graduate student?" I inquired severely. He gave a noncommittal nod. "One encounter should be enough to explain why you could not pay me to be a graduate student in America."

"I thought most of them were paid," said Hall. "Aren't there fellowships and stipends?"

"I'm talking about real money," I said tersely.

Krattenstein laughed and said, "James here is a true oddity. He doesn't want to go to law school and he doesn't want a Ph.D."

"I can't say I blame him about law school," Lidodes remarked, leaving unspoken his different feelings about the value of higher degrees in, say, Tudor constitutional history. "From what I've witnessed of my American students, Washington will one day resemble a courtroom, full of large Midwestern barristers from Michigan"—in English fashion he rhymed the first syllable with *pitch*—"talking a lot of bombastic nonsense."

"As opposed to university teachers," I said dryly, "who can be counted on to speak elegantly and write like Anglo-Saxon angels."

"Perhaps not in America," Lidodes said condescendingly, scoring rather nicely I thought, "but it is something we stress over here. Though I must admit it could be stressed even more to our post-graduate students. Some of them can't parse a simple sentence. It's hard to see why they are admitted. Yet they are, more every year."

"Are there any good ones?" asked Hall with a sycophant's sincerity. He could not have been more than thirty and there was something a little offensive about his question, or rather his manner in putting it. He might have been talking fish with a fellow angler—"any big ones?"

"A few," said Lidodes. "But they tend to be the quiet ones who get on with their work and keep their noses stuck deep in Bodley. Unless one's their supervisor, they tend to be virtually invisible. It's the difficult students that get heard about." He gestured tersely at Krattenstein. "Like the chap we were discussing."

"You know him," Krattenstein said to me.

"What?" I said, greatly puzzled. Could it be McCandles? As a graduate student, he was conspicuous only for his efforts to go unnoticed. In the shooting gallery of academic life, he was a duck that began every move across the line of supervisors' sights with its head already tucked under its wing.

"You know," said Krattenstein, raising a thick finger in the air, as if he expected the right name to alight on its tip. "The fellow you told me about at High Table, the one who made that scene during the lecture in Schools."

"Oh," I said in sudden comprehension, "you mean Newcastle."

"That's the one."

"You know him?" Lidodes asked dubiously.

"Well, sort of. I mean, I don't know him very well, He's not a friend or anything, but, well, I guess I know him." I imagine my hesitancy conveyed the sincerity of a *Daily Worker* columnist before the House Committee on Un-American Activities, denying any association with known communists. "Anyway," I said more lucidly, "what's he done now?" I realized that the "now" of this last sentence confirmed my acquaintance with the accused.

"God knows," said Lidodes bitterly. "He seems intent on pursuing a vendetta against one of our visitors."

"Visitors? You mean Lafayette Jackson."

"I'm not at liberty to say," Lidodes said sententiously, as if the Official Secrets Act extended farther afield from Whitehall than was generally known.

Krattenstein spoke up. "James knows all about it. He's the person who told me about Newcastle in the first place."

"Wait a minute," I said. "Please tell me what you're all talking about."

"We're not talking about anything," Lidodes snapped, "It's your friend who seems to be doing all the talking."

"He's not my friend," I said as calmly as I could. "But what's he been saying?"

"He's suggested in several conversations with faculty members that the work of Lafayette Jackson may be based on fraudulent scholarship. He's implied that her sources are some-how imaginary. Moreover, and with even less restraint, he's taken every possible occasion to attack the woman in print."

"I saw exactly one letter, in the *TLS*. It wasn't very nice, I'll grant you that, but then Newcastle isn't very nice. I can't see it doing any lasting damage to Lafayette Jackson."

Lidodes stood up and walked over to the magazine rack. He came back with a copy of the *New York Review of Books*, opened it to the letters page in the back, and thrust it into my lap. "I'm surprised you're not more *au courant* with the politics of literary journalism. Given your journalistic inter-lude in New York—it was New York, wasn't it?—I'd have thought you'd keep up more."

I ignored this and looked at the letter. It read:

Sir:

Que será será, or so Lafayette Jackson blithely suggests in her "musings" about El Salvador (NYRB, March 15). Yet omissions stud her remarks; if they disturb the care-ful reader it is with good reason, for these *lacunae* are either the product of deliberate distortion or appalling ignorance.

Most notable are the gaps in Ms. Jackson's discussion of the United Fruit Company's role in the turmoil of Salvadoran affairs in the 1950s. Although she writes at length about the U.S. House of Representatives subcom-mittee on Latin American affairs, nowhere does Ms. Jackson refer to the major conclusion of that committee's report of this past December: "American involvement in El Salvador's politics in the two decades since the Second World War must be seen through the lens of American corporate activity." Instead, Ms. Jackson re-peatedly cites the dissenting opinion of that report: "The role of the United Fruit Company in El Salvador has been repeatedly overstated."

This latter opinion comes from a minority of one,

whereas the majority report was signed by the sixteen other members of the committee with the full endorsement of the twenty-seven member staff. Nowhere is this fact alluded to by Ms. Jackson. Instead, under the guise of agnostic rumination, Ms. Jackson uses the arguments of a corporate and, in El Salvador's case, highly reactionary theology.

Although naturally no historian is immune from the historical and cultural forces of the Age ("No man is an island"), the perceptive reader is nonetheless left to make one of two conclusions: either Ms. Jackson, in the course of her researches, has mistaken the partisan propaganda of American business interests for objective documentation of political facts; or she has deliberately presented a partisan message clothed in the antiseptic garb of disinterested observation. If the former, Ms. Jackson has failed innocently but quite astonishingly as an historian and chronicler. If the latter conclusion applies, then she has cynically twisted the historian's tools to her own ideological ends. In either case, both her readers and the truth have been badly served.

Yours sincerely,

P. R. C. Newcastle
Christ Church, Oxford

Charles Bicker
Magdalen College, Oxford

Bicker! I thought to myself but refrained from admitting another damaging acquaintance. I looked up at Lidodes and said, "They don't mince words, I'll grant you that. But there's no real charge of fraud here, nothing about inventing sources."

Lidodes waved his hand impatiently. "Of course not. It's just the politicized ranting of juveniles. But the allusions are very disturbing."

"No man is an island," Krattenstein explained, and I looked back to the passage in the letter containing this phrase.

"What does that mean?"

"A quotation from Donne," said Lidodes. "The poet, John Donne. D, O, N, N, E."

"Thank you," I said heavily. "I was referring to the quotation's context in this letter."

"Ah," said Lidodes, then decided to enlighten me. "Mrs. Jackson's reputation, which is not inconsiderable according to some of your compatriots, rests to a large extent on a book she wrote about a plantation community on an island."

"I know that."

"I'm glad to hear it because until last month I certainly didn't. I hadn't even heard of Mrs. Jackson, not to mention her book." His tone suggested that he did not consider this a damaging admission.

"Is this the island Newcastle means in this letter?"

"What keen journalistic instincts you have," said Lidodes. Krattenstein looked uncomfortable about Lidodes' rudeness, but I was happy to tolerate it in order to hear the rest of the story. "The island is almost certainly one and the same," Lidodes continued, "although this Newcastle person has now told at least half my colleagues that the island never existed."

"What about her evidence? Doesn't she quote letters from the island's owner?"

"In exhaustive detail. Newcastle has accordingly cast aspersions on the authenticity of the letters."

"Is he right?"

For the first time Lidodes looked more weary than annoyed. But then irritation returned to his voice and he spoke animatedly. "Almost certainly not. He has produced no evidence of worth. But why is he so interested in the matter anyway?"

"It's his field."

"Strange in itself, I should have thought. But given the oddity of his professional preoccupation, why does he presume to try to interest others in it? I mean really, whom does he hope to have judge such an accusation here? This is an English university, not an American 'college.' This is Oxford, not the University of Baton Rouge. We make no pretense to authority in historical exotica. There is only one Civil War that draws our attention here." I realized suddenly how angry Lidodes was, for despite his conventional anti-American snobbery he was a scholar and would never normally say anything this stupid. But in heated fashion he now continued, "What would young Newcastle like us to do? Call in some expert from Bodley? There aren't any in this area. Ring up Rhodes House Library?"

I found this so silly that I said snidely, "Rhodes House *is* part of Bodley."

Lidodes threw both hands in the air in exasperation. I hadn't meant to inflame him further but I was clearly blowing on a well-stoked fire; it was too late for amends. He stood up and got his coat. "Perhaps Rhodes House is to you," he said slowly. Then he said good night to Krattenstein and Hall and walked out of the room.

For a moment none of us said anything. Hall looked mildly embarrassed and he soon made mumbled apologies and left. I heard him in the courtyard a minute later, calling after his older colleague. Krattenstein looked at me for a moment and said, "You shouldn't be so hard on him."

"Who? On Lidodes? You must be joking. He'd chew me up and spit me out for breakfast if I let him. Besides, what he was saying is ridiculous."

I went and poured myself another lager. When I sat down again Krattenstein said, "Lidodes has problems with Lafayette Jackson."

"Tell me why," I said curtly.

"He is her host while she's at Oxford. Newcastle's antics aren't making his job any easier."

"What do you mean, her host? Since when does Oxford provide seeing-eye dogs for visitors? You know this place: if Pierre Trudeau were invited to visit All Souls as a Fellow for a year he'd only find the place by asking the policeman at Carfax for directions."

"It's not Lafayette Jackson herself; it's her connections. A committee was formed last year to promote American Studies at Oxford. It's got dons and American businessmen, and all sorts of important people on it."

"And Lafayette's on the committee. Big deal."

"No, no. Listen to me. The committee's trying to raise money for a new library just for American Studies. Last year they received a major gift of letters and journals written by Robert E. Lee. They are supposed to be housed in the new library and they've obviously been a great selling point in attracting donations for the building."

"So?"

"The papers were originally bought by a rich friend of the library from a bookseller in New Orleans named Smiley."

"I recognize the name."

"Yes, well Smiley is a close friend of Howard Jackson and was also the source of the correspondence Lafayette discovered for her book. You know, the plantation owner's letters. The committee is hoping to buy (if they can't get them given) these letters; as a result, they're being very nice to Smiley's friend, Lafayette Jackson. But now Newcastle is claiming that both the letters Jackson quotes and the Lee papers are phony."

"I'm not surprised." Actually the news impressed me. It is one thing to be told privately of someone's eccentric convictions (as McCandles had told me of Newcastle's), quite another to find them public currency.

"And it's Lidodes' job to show Jackson around and keep her happy. With things like the little dinner tonight. They should never have chosen him: to begin with, he doesn't much like Americans, and he's also skeptical about this new library—you know Lidodes, he thinks the money should go for a center on The Wars of the Roses. But he's a member of the faculty, his colleagues tell him it's important, so he grits his teeth and does the best he can. Think of how much he had in common with Howard Jackson and you can see how much he's enjoying all this. And then some little graduate student comes along and says the woman is a fake, without any evidence at all I might add, and Lidodes feels he has to defend her. It's most uncomfortable for him."

"The whole thing is fairly ironic," I said, and Krattenstein frowned. "Oh come on," I said, "I grew up in this racket, it's what my father does. I'm not any good at it myself but I spent my childhood watching academics cutting each other's throats for various kinds of advancement. It's completely fallacious to think they're any different from anybody else. They have the same ambitions, the same envy, the same lust, the same charlatans in their midst."

"And scholarship doesn't enter into it? You're that cynical?"

"Of course I'm not. Look, it's like academic novels— they're practically a genre in themselves. If all you knew of academic life was what you read in those novels you'd probably conclude that the only thing professors do is drink and chase their colleagues' wives around the kitchen table. Every three chapters there's a brief sentence saying, 'And then he graded papers for an hour.' That's a false picture, obviously, but pictures have to be false if they're going to be interesting. Political thrillers don't tend to discuss Federal milk subsidies, either."

"So what are you trying to say?" Krattenstein asked impatiently.

"Just that the drama of all this is interesting. Even very funny in parts."

"And the truth doesn't enter into it."

"On the contrary, I'm starting to wonder if what Newcastle is saying isn't true. Lidodes doesn't seem to care what the truth is."

"I care," said Krattenstein defensively, "but I doubt very much that Newcastle has anything to go on. All he's doing is smearing the reputations of Smiley and Jackson. He hasn't proved anything. None of his letters so far even discuss this. He's just going around gossiping—there's even something in *Cherwell* this week, but it's not by Newcastle. If you ask me, he's being malicious to the point of dementia."

"Look who's being charitable now. A minute ago you wanted me to feel for Lidodes because he's got 'mixed feelings.' Now you're saying Newcastle's a dangerous lunatic. You're not showing much compassion there."

"He's trying to ruin other people's careers. Until he produces some hard evidence his behavior is indefensible."

I did not reply for I did not want to be put in the position of defending Newcastle. His behavior *had* been needlessly provocative, not that this surprised me. The fact that he had written two letters on utterly unrelated topics was no coincidence but rather the manifestation of a grudge. And if he were making the much more serious charge of fraud (his letters argued only incompetence and right-wing views) then he would have to support them with evidence. I knew this; Krattenstein knew this; so there was no point arguing over it. Thus, when Krattenstein spoke again he simply asked about my work. We discussed my coming exams for a few minutes, but there was a certain constraint between us now, created by Lidodes' outburst, and soon Krattenstein excused himself and left the common room. I stayed there, reading an old copy of *Private Eye* and drinking more beer. Then I watched half of a Gene Kelly movie with some undergraduates in the television room downstairs. On the way to my room, I stopped at the Lodge and picked up a copy of *Cherwell*, the student newspaper, dropping my five pence with a clank into the box.

Back in my room I noticed that it was after one o'clock; the street beneath my window was quiet and dark. I drank a tumbler of sherry while I flipped through the paper. I found the item easily enough, just after John Evelyn, the paper's gossip column. It read:

> The status of a new Oxford library for American Studies is now in doubt following revelations that documents bought last spring, intended for the new library's shelves, from a distinguished American dealer in Southern historical items are of questionable authenticity.

> Latest reports suggest that the valuable nature of this acquisition may be literally *Gone With the Wind*.

> Embarrassment has been increased by the presence in Oxford this term of a visiting American don whose reputation rests almost exclusively on the "discovery" of papers also emanating from the same "T. J. Wise" of New Orleans. The researches of one *Bituminosos Ferens* threaten, in American lingo, to blow both dealer and don out of the historical water, leaving Oxford with a new source of foolscap and with mud on the blueprints for its new library.

Bituminosos Ferens took me a minute to decipher since my classical education, as I've mentioned, was confined to genetic residue. But I did not need my father to translate this: "Carrying Coals" could only refer to Newcastle. I found myself thinking that he had better find some evidence and pretty quickly, too. Then I thought about Celia and when I would see her next. How long did her Japanese tours take? I went to my desk and found a postcard of a map of England in the Bodleian which Carol, my ex-girlfriend, had said looked like a phallus. Possibly Celia would like it more. I addressed the postcard and in tipsy handwriting wrote:

> We velly pleased with tour of Bath. Now we in Oxford where by stlange coincidence we met charming Amelican boy who say he know you. He velly good news.
>
> Best Legards,
>
> Wantowa Seeyousoonawa

The word "puerile" flickered into my drunken head. I threw away the card, took a fresh one, and wrote:

> I hope you have survived the demands of your visitors from the East. You will be pleased to hear that I am working hard for my exams. It would be a great set-back to my new and hard-won maturity if it was not rewarded by a visit from you when my ordeal is over. Please come. J.

Eleven

Throughout my childhood, Sunday was the nadir of the week, twenty-four hours stained too deep for enjoyment by contemplation of the Monday certainty called School. Football on television, going to the movies, visits to my grandmother—no activity served to ease my dread as the clock ticked and the world moved inexorably towards Monday morning.

Oxford changed this. My tutorials had been few and sprinkled lightly through the week; now that exams approached, even these minimal requirements ceased, and Sunday was no different at all. No different, that is, in its burdens on me, for in fact Sunday is uniquely quiet in Oxford. On Saturday, the town center fills with tourists and shoppers, and the tight frame of what originated as a medieval town swells to bursting point. Sundays the balloon deflates, the only activity in city center a few tight bands of church-goers, light-suited and bright-hatted in the new spring air.

I rose late, showered, and tried to work in my room. In the pub up the street, I ate a lunch of shepherd's pie and warm bitter, then went and read the Sunday papers in the common room. Unlike the Sunday *New York Times*, the English papers can be read in an hour. Even detailed examination of the financial pages and a run through the lowliest cricket results only let me stretch things to an hour and a half. I returned reluctantly to my room to work some more. Exams began in just two weeks, and I was showing unusual application in my efforts to avoid a Third. I had a hack journalist's facility for turning a phrase, and armed with this and a few of the more obvious philosophical arguments I started to feel I might just make it through the coming trials.

Late that afternoon a knock on my door relieved me with the prospect of company. I opened the door and discovered McCandles' fiancée, Audrey, standing outside visibly upset.

"Hi," I said, startled to see her. We were not friends: I found her cold and a little stuffy; she seemed to hold no great affection for me, either. She was not so naive to think that I—or anyone—was a corrupting influence on McCandles, but she nevertheless seemed to resent my unfailing cooperation in helping her fiancé evoke his demonic side. She had also made it clear to McCandles that she was not prepared to encourage my feelings for Celia, which I had confided to him, presumably (this McCandles would only imply) because I was not "right" for her. Yet despite our mutual reservations, Audrey and I managed to maintain a reasonably cordial truce. I had never seen her emotional.

"Can I come in?" she asked a little nervously. I don't think she had ever set foot in my room.

"Of course. I thought you and Wilmarth were in London. Don't you have to work tomorrow?" She worked in a pub, a lowly job considering her background, but the only employment she could find without working papers.

"I do," she said, sitting on my low reclining chair while I perched on the bed. "But I came back with Wilmarth this morning."

"Coffee?" I offered, remembering my manners. Audrey

always made me very conscious of my manners. "I can heat some water."

"No thank you," she said stiffly, trying to sit up straight, an impossibility in that chair. She was a short girl, about McCandles' height, with a fine head of wavy auburn hair. The legs below her dress showed the first effects of spring sun, slightly flushed but not yet tan. I made myself stop looking at them.

"Why did you come back so early?" I asked, trying to make conversation until she said whatever she had on her mind. "Where's Bicker?" I added.

"He's still in London," she said, but that seemed all she was confident of relating, and an awkward silence ensued.

"Well," I said, standing up and moving to the sink, "what did you do in London?" I poured us each a glass of sherry and put her glass on the table beside her.

"The usual," she said quietly, but with a bitterness in her voice. I suddenly realized she was about to cry. Her chin, usually a WASP Gibraltar, now wobbled perilously.

"Did you win?" I asked as gently as possible.

She shook her head tightly and two tears popped like raindrops out of one eye. I thought it was tactful to ignore them. "How much did you lose?" I asked, again as gently as possible. I like to think I can assume a delicate doctor-like manner when coping with the distressed, but tears from Audrey's other eye now joined the original two and soon shiny streams curled along her cheeks. I got a tissue and waited while she blew her nose.

"I kept telling him we should leave," she said sniffling, "but he wouldn't go. He kept saying he'd win it back."

"Was he playing roulette?"

"Is that the one with the wheel?" When I nodded she nodded, too.

"So how much did he lose?"

"Almost four hundred pounds," she said, then started crying again.

I had to suppress a smile. McCandles had money of his own, so there was little prospect of his washing dishes to clear the debt, or of tuxedoed thugs motoring to Christ Church to break his legs. He could afford to lose money gambling; after a few disastrous attempts to compete, I had given up trying to match his bets.

"Audrey, I know it's a lot," I said patiently, "but he can afford it. You won't end up in the poorhouse." Their wedding was scheduled for July, at Audrey's parents' house in Maine, and I wondered briefly if she were scared that the reception would now have to held at Burger King. Audrey was a New Englander with the unpretentious manner of ten generations of town meetings and nonconformist chapel, but she had a latent love of luxury as well, a softer opulent layer beneath the flint façade, and I suspected this sneaking lust for life's good things had bloomed under McCandles' expansive tutelage. America's Southern aristocracy seemed to have no counterpart to the New England dowager who wore old tennis shoes and had three million dollars in bonds under the back stairs. Southern people saw nothing tasteful in disguising wealth, clearly an attitude Audrey would need to get used to.

But now she said, "It's not the money that bothers me."

"It's not?" I replied in surprise.

"No. It's Wilmarth."

"Why? What's wrong with him?"

She sipped her sherry, then said, "You know his moods. He's always moody. But right now he's so depressed, more than I've ever seen before. I came back with him because I was scared to leave him alone." She repeated, "I've never seen him like this before. When we got back here he just sat in his room and wouldn't say anything to me. He's been like that ever since we left the casino. I had to dissuade him from coming back here last night. And he hardly slept."

I had seen McCandles depressed before, but this sounded unprecedented. "Where is he now?" I asked.

"In his room."

"Is he drinking?"

"I don't think so. He's just sitting there."

I stood up and put on my coat. It was a down jacket I'd bought in Michigan and I liked to wear it, for it reminded me of the place in America I most enjoyed. "You stay here," I said to Audrey. "I'll go talk to him. Don't worry, he's probably just down because of the money. The problem with gambling is that once the money's gone, there's nothing to show for it. That can be very depressing."

It was a sunny day but still cool, with a breeze that seemed to threaten the juvenile leaves struggling for a foothold on the trees outside college. I took the long way to McCandles' rooms through the memorial garden where the first flower plantings lined the earth, sitting up like small, colorful buoys in a sea of soil. It was the type of day we often have in the Midwest, when a false spring brings enough balmy air to deceive you into thinking the warm weather has arrived. In Michigan, I used to untie my baseball glove, bound for the winter in twine and soaked in neat's-foot oil, knowing that spring was on its way. In England, winter was over, but there was, as always, no guarantee of a real spring before summer.

I found McCandles sitting in one of his deep armchairs, apparently lost in thought. His door was wide open and he gave only a mild wave when I came in. He was dressed in a Sunday suit and a sombre blue tie. He looked as if he were in a law firm's lobby, awaiting an interview with the senior partner.

"Hi," I said, sitting down to face him. McCandles nodded. "Why are you all dressed up?"

He looked down at his tie and trousers and shrugged. "I don't know. I suppose because it's Sunday. At home I was always forced to dress up on Sundays."

"For church?"

He shook his head. "To go to my great aunt's. We had Sunday lunch with her most weeks. And a very bad meal it was, too. Chicken and rice, chicken and potatoes, sometimes just chicken on its own. And only water to drink. She was a Baptist."

"Is she still alive?"

"Of course not. Nobody in my family's still alive. Except my parents, and the way they drink I don't give them much time, either. Some Sundays they'd want a drink so bad they'd send me to my aunt's alone."

"Well, I wouldn't call it Dickensian, but you do make it sound pretty grim."

For the first time animation came into his voice. "It *was* grim." He paused and said, "I feel awful low."

"I know. Audrey told me."

"She came to see you?"

"Yes. She's in my room right now." I took the risk of offending him. "She told me about the gambling. She said you'd lost a lot."

"It's only money," said McCandles irritably. "I don't now why she's so worried. God knows, I'm no good at the stock market, but after law school I'm certain to make lots of money. I don't see myself working for Legal Aid, do you?"

I laughed and said no. "Are you looking forward to law school?" I added.

He shook his head again. "Not really. It should be interesting to work hard for a change, but I can't say I'm looking forward to it. Especially now that it's certain I'm going."

"When wasn't it certain?"

McCandles shrugged. "I don't know. I had a recurring

fantasy that I'd forget about law school and go home. I'd farm with my father, take over the plantation—that's what it is, you know, I don't know why my father even bothers to call it a farm—perhaps even run for Congress. I went so far as to write my father about it."

"What did your father say?"

"I got the letter on Friday. He says indeed it is a fantasy, however much it recurs. I should attend law school and erase all thoughts of returning home."

"Why did he say that?"

"Who knows? He never liked me that much."

"Come off it. He's your father."

"I suppose he is, though in the South you can't always be sure. Actually, I think he just believes I'd be miserable. That I wouldn't fit in."

"Is he right?"

McCandles looked over at one of his pictures. It was a small Rowlandson he had found near Golden Square in London, a watercolor of three fox hunters drinking after the hunt, the fox presumably dispatched, the hounds returned. One of the hunters had just broken his chair; his two pals were howling with laughter as he sat collapsed on the floor with a drunken expression of outrage on his fat red face.

"Yes," McCandles said slowly, "he's right. I've been away too long. Prep school, then college, then here—it's too long a separation. They still know me down there, but I could never really be part of them again."

"Are things that clannish?"

"In the deep South? Yes. I mean, suppose you wanted to live there, God knows why, but let's say you did. You could settle there, do perfectly well. You'd always know that you weren't from there, but I guess that would be true anywhere you went except Michigan. With me, it's different. I am from there, and yet I'm not any longer. That's a difficult position, if you see what I mean. I could act like them most of the time, but let's face it, I dress differently now, I read books, I drink vodka sometimes—all sorts of eccentric behavior I'd either have to swear off or else stick out like a renegade. And the religious question—that in itself would cause problems. I can't pretend anymore. I don't know if I'll be a Catholic or not, but I'm certainly no Baptist."

"What about Audrey?"

"What about her? She'd live there if I asked her to, but that's just another problem. If only she weren't so Boston." He waved his hand in disgust. "Anyway, this is all irrelevant. I'll be in law school next year, surrounded by one hundred and fifty of the best and the brightest."

"You'll like New Haven," I lied. "It's not a bad town. And it's close to New York."

"That's an attraction?" McCandles said sarcastically. He added wistfully, "I wish I'd got into Harvard. I don't really care, it's all the same to me. But Audrey would have liked it; half her family's there."

"She'll like New Haven, and she'll get a job."

McCandles wasn't listening. "Did I tell you that I found out why I didn't get into Harvard?"

"No."

"One of Audrey's cousins works in the Admissions Office. He discovered that one of the recommendations wasn't very good. Guess which one."

"Which?"

"Hubert. Harvard was the only law school that required a letter from my Oxford supervisor. I thought Hubert liked me."

"Do you know what he wrote?"

"I know it wasn't very positive. When I think about it, I suppose I shouldn't be surprised. I ate lunch with Hubert just after he wrote the letter, and I remember him saying he thought it would be a miracle if I got into Harvard. That sounded a little strange, but I simply thought he was being English about it—you know what they think about American letters of recommendation."

"It doesn't matter," I said.

"Sure it matters," he said without annoyance, as if he simply wanted to keep the record straight.

I changed the subject. "Have you seen Newcastle lately?"

"On Thursday. Why?"

I told McCandles of my encounter the evening before with Lafayette Jackson and of the details explained by Krattenstein. It turned out that McCandles knew all about it.

"I was surprised to find Bicker's name on the letter," I said.

"Why? He and Newcastle are bosom pals."

"Really? Since when?"

"The last few weeks. Certainly since Bicker's talk. They've established a radical alliance. The young Trotskys of Oxford."

"Well, all I can say is that Newcastle had better put up or shut up about Lafayette."

"He's working on it, or so he told me Thursday. He didn't tell me what he's doing but I wouldn't underestimate him. Don't forget his talent for research."

"He'd better hurry up, if only for his sake. Lidodes was very angry. I wouldn't be surprised if they threw Newcastle out of here if he doesn't prove these charges."

"No great loss to him, I would think. Or to Oxford."

"What would Newcastle do next?"

"How do I know?" McCandles said shortly. "Emigrate to Australia. What else does everybody do over here? Either they go on the dole or they leave, just like we're going to leave."

"Yes," I said irritably, "but we're not English. You have a future where you're going."

McCandles grew sarcastic. "Yes, of course I have everything in the world to look forward to back in America. The ample material rewards of the New World." He grew more serious. "But you know something? I don't want to go back home. I can't help it."

"I don't want to go back either. I like it here."

"I don't know how much I like it here; I'm simply certain that I'm not going to like it *there* very much. And what are you going to do when you go back? Journalism again?" He said this with scorn, since he held decisive, English-like views about journalism, and he was not impressed by the profession's new-found cachet in America.

"I guess so. What else can I do? But I can't say I'm excited by the prospect. Studying Philosophy and Politics has been a mistake. All it's done is make me no longer want to be a journalist. To tell you the truth, I'm starting to think I should have written a thesis. Part of me would still like to write a thesis—or something substantial anyway—and stay here."

McCandles, influenced by his own unfinished work, dismissed this out of hand with a scoff and shake of his head. "Why not work for one of those consulting outfits? Your degree will be in PPE; you could get a job."

"But I don't know anything about economics."

"I hope you don't think economists do, either. If you were to read ten back issues of the *Economist* you could fake it along with the best of them. You could make *lots* of money." McCandles' eyes gleamed for the first time.

"I'd be bored stiff. And I'd have to live in New York. No money could make it worthwhile, especially since I'd know I was a fake."

"Oh," said McCandles snidely, "and your integrity's intact as a journalist. 'Tell me, Senator,' " McCandles said in booming, parodic tones, " 'how does your wife feel after her mastectomy?' 'Excuse me, Mr. President, can you explain your wife's recent assignation with Chancellor Adenauer during the GATT talks?' Come off it: don't tell me you can live with yourself doing that crap, or that it's deeply exciting and valuable. Sally Archimedes may be able to delude herself—she writes so badly I suppose she has to—but don't you go giving me that line."

"I know," I said half-despairingly. No one could depress me like McCandles. "I came over here to cheer you up," I said angrily, "and all you've done is to make *me* feel depressed."

McCandles laughed for the first time. "This is what the Freudians call transference. I feel better now. Let's have a drink."

In the week before my exams began I avoided McCandles. Bicker was also taking Schools but he approached them with an attitude so relentlessly blasé that I couldn't bear to talk with him. "Relax," he kept saying, "you can always walk out if you can't stand it." But I couldn't walk out, for I was starting to realize that an acceptable result in Finals might let me do what I now wanted to do—stay at Oxford. There was no point confiding further in McCandles on this point: I had begun to realize that although his cynicism was fully democratic (for it never hesitated to deflate his own ambitions), this did not make it any less wounding when applied like a hot iron to my own aspirations.

Exams began on the last Friday in May and not even the surprise of a note from Hopkins, asking me to see him Tuesday morning in his rooms, distracted me from a growing fear that I would be consumed by nerves well before the Final Performance commenced. Remorse filled me at all hours; my two years at Oxford seemed utterly wasted; my previous dedication to personal enjoyment was entirely supplanted by vows of future temperance and hard work. This form of near-panic was not peculiar to me; through all the college quads that week walked legions of the dilatory, now newly penitent. But the communion of our misery did not allay its harsh and individual effect. I was scared.

Hopkins sensed this at once. He shoved a large glass of sherry into my hand and told me to sit next to the fire.

"Do you know," I said with an immoderate laugh that only fuelled my nerves, "this is the first drop of anything a tutor's ever offered me. Before I came here my image of dons was that they fed you on a perpetual diet of dry sherry and dry wit."

"And you've found both in poor supply?" he asked with jerky twitches.

I laughed in embarrassment. "Let's just say that my preconceptions were slightly off base."

"Have you enjoyed yourself here?"

"Immensely," I said, and realized self-consciously that in America I would have used a different word.

"It's often hard to tell with you Americans. For so many of you Oxford seems a pointless interlude. I mean, two years here, then back to the law—law school I think you call it. I often wonder why they bother."

"So do I."

"Are you doing that?"

"Law school. No."

"Have you a job lined up?" When I shook my head he seemed a little puzzled. "Didn't you work in America before you came here? You aren't one of those people who came straight from one university to another, are you?"

"I worked for a while in New York. Then I came here."

"Will you go back to New York?"

I shrugged. "Not if I can help it. I'm actually starting to think I'd like to stay here, if there's any way to do it."

"At Oxford?" he asked as if caught off guard. I nodded.

"To do another degree?" I nodded again.

"In Philosophy?" he asked in horrified tones.

"Good God no," I said quickly. "In English."

"Oh," he said with palpable relief. "And for how long have you wanted to do this?"

I sat for a minute thinking. How long had it been? I wasn't sure myself. "I suppose I really made up my mind about fifteen minutes ago," I said. Hopkins laughed. I continued, more seriously, "It *is* a recent decision, but in a way it's the obvious choice. You see, all my interests are literary, all the reading I actually like to do. I read English at college in the States and, frankly, it's all I'm any good at. I did Politics and Philosophy here in an effort to widen my horizons, whatever that means. Only I guess it didn't take."

"Can you afford it? The fees are very steep."

"I don't know. There're loans: but I'd probably have to work part-time."

"I see," said Hopkins thoughtfully. "And what if you can't do another degree?"

"I guess I'd have to go back to journalism," I said, suddenly depressed at the prospect. "In New York," I added, feeling more depressed.

"What's wrong with that?" Hopkins asked, but not challengingly.

"Nothing, I suppose, if that's what you want to do. I mean if that's what *one* wants to do. But I'm not sure I could bear it, not after having stopped journalism for two years. It suddenly seems so trivial. It's either malicious and gossipy— that's the interesting side—or else it's pompous and inflated with its self-importance. It just seems such a waste to me. I mean, there are literally thousands of Americans my age who are dying to be journalists. Well, why not let them take my place? I'd rather do something else with my life."

"Some might question the value of writing a thesis, too, you know."

"I understand that. I'm not saying that there's anything more valuable about doing post-graduate work than working for a magazine. Frankly, neither is going to win the Albert Schweitzer Award for contributions to humanity. It's simply that, as far as I'm concerned, I want to do something of value to me. If three people I respected like my thesis, that's enough for me. And it would mean more to me than a by-line in a rag three million people read."

I shut up at this point and waited for Hopkins to reply. Even after two years of his tutoring, I could not begin to gauge or predict his reactions. Yet what appealed to me about him was that I could rely on him to be honest. If it were clear to one and all that I was cut out only for journalism, that life intended me to be a male Sally Archimedes, then Hopkins would have no hesitation in telling me so. Behind the sharp, occasionally unfriendly façade, beneath the layer of facial tics, the blinking eyes, and rapid, nervous hand movements, he was a straightforward and perceptive man. He said now, after a lengthy pause, "If I remember correctly you did rather well in America." He stopped as if to consider whether this could possibly be true. He seemed to decide that, on the whole, it might well have been the case. "I should think you'd stand a chance of being accepted here for English. *If*," and the word loomed large, "you don't cock up your Finals." He stared at me as if to dampen the hope rising in me. "A Third would be disastrous."

"Yes, I know," I said, slightly chastened.

"You're going to need a very good Second Class degree. I think we can safely assume that a First is out of the question. It's not as if you did a lot of work over the last two years." He leaned back against the mantel and looked down at me. "But to be candid, that doesn't always have much to do with how one performs in Schools. In a sense, they are simply strange, archaic exercises we still insist upon. It's often possible to do quite well in them regardless of the amount of work one's done."

I must have shown surprise at this, for during the past two years Hopkins and my other tutors had devoted most of their efforts to telling me the contrary. Seeing the look on my face, Hopkins said, "I know, I've always told you to work hard or you'd do badly. That may well turn out to be the case. But there's no point harping on your inactivity—not if you now want to stay on here. And from what the Politics dons say, you could do rather well in those papers. Philosophy," he added in less friendly fashion, "is a different story. You have a penchant for facile, glib analyses that are usually quite wrong. I should use lots of these in the Politics papers—the examiners will consider them provocative. But avoid them at all costs in the Philosophy examinations. Tell them what little you know and be content with that." He paused, uncertain about what note on which to end his counsel, and threw his hands up into the air. "Who knows? You might just pull it off."

Well, at least he hadn't written me off completely, and I wanted to convey my thanks for that. But he cut me short. "Now you must be going. Your colleague Michael Shambling is in the infirmary with a bad case of pre-Schools jitters. It's one of my duties to help him get his nerve back." He drank off his sherry and moved me out the door. "If I have to carry the little bugger into Schools myself, I'll still make sure he gets there."

Twelve

I had approached Schools feeling they were meaningless, the results no more than Greek marks on a script I'd never see again. Suddenly, however, this had been changed by my new desire to stay on at Oxford. Was it too late? There was no point thinking any more about the amount of work I hadn't done for two years or there would be no end to an orgy of regret that would guarantee a disastrous performance in my exams. Instead, I turned a deaf ear to Bicker and McCandles' entreaties to come get drunk and tried to do two years worth of reading in three days. Hegel's political philosophy I did in four hours (who in any case would want to do more?), and Mill was neatly summarized by a quick perusal of the pertinent section in a second-hand book I bought called *Fifty Great Thinkers*. Having once written a 5,000 word feature article on liquid natural gas in the course of a weekend, I felt well-trained for the last-minute nature of my work. But the stakes seemed infinitely higher.

By Friday morning I was sleepless and inflamed with tension, a pitch of energy that geared still higher as I walked down the High in the subfusc uniform of dark suit and white bow-tie, joining the other undergraduates as we filtered through the colorful commerce of the Oxford market and merged into a black-and-white checkerboard of anticipation outside the Examination Schools. I had a quotation from Quine in my head and a postcard from Celia in my hand. It showed a porcelain jar from some Chinese dynasty, and she had written on the back: "Thank you for your card. If I can survive the Japanese, you can survive Schools. You had better, or my trip to Oxford will be wasted. C." So she was going to meet me when I was through; elated, I walked into my exams.

At five o'clock that afternoon I stumbled out of Schools, feeling like fresh chopped meat. I had worked densely, insistently, through two philosophy exams, but my sense of accomplishment was swamped by my depression at the thought of six more exams to come. I looked for Bicker in the throng but couldn't spot him, so I started back towards college, taking the long way, along the cobbled pavements of Merton Street to the lane of cherry trees that ran down to Christ Church Meadow. The trees were near the end of their blossom and I thought of Michigan, where soon the sour cherries would be in harvest. I followed the wall along the Meadow and stopped to watch some schoolboys in shorts playing cricket. One boy bowled and another swung and missed and collapsed with a howl as the ball knocked his wicket down. I moved on, past the Fellows Garden, towards the turn for my college and home. On a bench stuck smack in the middle of the long walk sat Newcastle, his body cramped up as if in seizure while he wrote furiously on notecards held against an opened book.

Before I even thought about it, I called out a greeting. He barely acknowledged it; piqued, I walked over to the bench. He seemed to finish a sentence as I came up behind him. Noticing me, he put down his cards and the book. The latter was a copy of a book called *An Enquiry into the Nature of Certain Nineteenth Century Pamphlets*. McCandles owned a copy and called it simply "Carter and Pollard" after its two authors. I knew only that it was a book about books and about fraud, the two subjects dearest to McCandles' heart.

"Working?" I asked.

"Yes," he said abruptly, "working very hard indeed. Have you seen McCandles?"

"He's not in his rooms?" They were only a stone's throw from where he sat.

"No, and I must speak with him." Newcastle flicked hair out of his eyes and surveyed me. "Schools?" he asked.

"My first day. I just got out."

"What a waste of time," he said sharply. "It's such a fascist system; some day soon someone's going to do away with the whole elitist sham."

I didn't need to hear this just then, so to change the subject I asked Newcastle what he was working on.

"Something of a revelation," he said with an air of smug mystery. "It should go a long way towards setting things right."

"Setting what right?"

"Certain deceptions, certain lies made by one of your countrymen and swallowed whole by this university. I think I've caught him dead to rights."

"Who are you talking about?"

"A bookseller. Not much of a bookseller, I should add, but the implications of his exposure will be very great indeed. He's not the only one whose reputation will sink."

I was intrigued but also so tired after my exams that I was uncertain how to press him further. "Are you *certain?*" I said weakly.

"Ninety-nine per cent. There's a general meeting of members next week. I'll have something to show them then. Something explosive."

"Members of what?" I asked.

He looked impatient with my ignorance. "The Friends of

the new American Studies Library. It's run by the same crowd who brought the Robert E. Lee papers here. Surely you know what they are. The *supposed* Robert E. Lee papers."

"They really are fakes?"

"Almost unquestionably. And the proof," he said confidently, picking up Carter & Pollard, "should be in my hands Monday week."

"When's this meeting?"

"That Friday, of course," he said as if I'd been trying to catch him out. "You should attend."

"It's the day I finish Schools. You'll have to tell me about it afterwards."

"Don't worry. You'll hear all about it. It will make the respectable dailies."

This seemed a little pompous. "Not the *Sun*? Don't you want this on page three next to the dolly bird's tits?"

"That's not inconceivable, should my findings have a personal as well as public effect. With any luck they will."

"Personal effect on whom?"

"Lafayette Jackson. Another of your countrymen—I should say countrywomen. Not that I hold that against her. I wouldn't be entirely surprised if she thought of suicide after all this comes out."

"Newcastle, forgive my dimness, but why will she care? What do the Robert E. Lee papers have to do with her? She didn't write them—even if Lee didn't either."

"No, she didn't," he admitted grudgingly.

"So what is the connection? Why will she be devastated by your findings?"

"Smiley," said Newcastle, smiling himself so that for a moment I was confused. Then I realized he meant the New Orleans bookseller, Howard Jackson's friend. "He supplied the Lee papers," Newcastle continued, "he sold them, he vouched for their authenticity."

"Yes?" I said to draw him out further. Newcastle could suddenly clam up, and I didn't want that to happen now.

"Lafayette's island, her miraculous documents, the letters in her book. They come from Smiley, too."

From my conversation with Krattenstein I knew what he was getting at, but I must have not reacted, for Newcastle grew impatient. "Don't you see? The letters she says she found through Smiley are too good to be true. She's trying to sell them to Oxford, just like the Lee papers were sold. But if the Lee papers are fakes, who's going to want her island letters? Same dealer, same period, same unpleasant smell. Even if her letters *are* real, no one's going to be very sure of it. There will simply be no way to remove the suggestion that the letters may be fake, not once everyone knows that the Lee papers are fraudulent. Oxford won't buy them, no library will. And there will always be a taint to her reputation. The game, as you Americans say, is almost over for Mrs. Jackson."

He spoke with extraordinarily explicit relish. I knew now it was not pedantry that drove him. "That's what matters to you, doesn't it?" I asked him. "You don't care about the Lee papers, not really. You only want to show they're fake because of how it will affect Lafayette Jackson. *That's* what matters to you."

"Precisely," he said, as if I had finally caught on.

"But *why* do you care so much? Because she wouldn't be your adviser? Because you've decided she was once rude to you? So what? Hubert's been rude to everybody. Why don't you go after him? Why her?"

"I'm not sure you'd understand."

"Try me. I'm a very understanding kind of guy."

"Don't you see?" he said eagerly. "This woman's commonly thought of as an eminent historian. Her views are taken seriously on all sorts of topics, merely because of one very narrow book she's written. The political impact of this is quite enormous, and unfortunate. She has a forum for all sorts of silly opinions. Everything she writes is published in a prominent journal."

"While serious students like you have to work hard just to get by."

"Yes," said Newcastle agreeably, surprised by my astuteness.

"Fair enough," I said, not thinking it fair at all. "But what about your own work? You must be spending all your time on this. Aren't you going to finish your thesis?"

"It will have to wait," he said solemnly and laid a pale hand on Carter & Pollard. "This is more important."

I pointed to the book. "What does Hubert think about what you're doing?"

"You think I'd tell him? He's chiefly responsible for acquiring the Robert E. Lee papers. He's going to look fairly foolish, as well. Besides, he and that woman are thick as thieves."

"So what will you do after this exposé?"

"Ah," he said with a smile. He stood up and collected his papers and together we started to walk down the gravel promenade that led to the arch and McCandles' rooms. "I don't think Oxford is the best place to pursue this kind of research. Too many vested interests. Too much dining at High Table and too little scholarship. I think I may find it more useful to do my work elsewhere."

Well, I thought, at least he understands his neck is in the noose, too. I wondered how much he knew of the anger he had provoked; if Lidodes was annoyed, what did Hubert feel? If Newcastle had some glimmering of this, then I had just been told a highly inventive account of his own imminent expulsion. You had to admire his balls.

We drew to a halt by the Christ Church arch. "I see McCandles is in," said Newcastle, pointing to the light in his rooms. Even in bright sunshine, McCandles liked to flood them with artificial light. He once confessed to me that he slept with his bedside lamp on, a vestigial habit from his childhood.

"Are you going to see him?" I asked.

"Yes. I know he'll want to hear what I've been up to. Aren't you coming in?"

I hesitated. "I don't think I will," I said finally. I left Newcastle and walked through the Memorial Gardens to my college. I felt as I once had after visiting my grandfather in a nursing home. It was a month before his death; his body had almost completely given out and his wits were half-gone. He remained coherent enough to make conversation possible but exhausting. Everything he said made perfect sense to him, virtually none to me. When I left him, I had to struggle to leave the eerie world of his half-right mind and resurrect the tenuous grip I have on my own.

When I returned to college I found a special delivery letter from the States in my box. I suddenly felt very tired; after my encounter with Newcastle I was not prepared for any bad news from home. I took the letter back to my room and poured myself a whiskey. Drinking it off, I refilled my glass and sat down to read the letter. It was from my grandfather's lawyer and golfing partner, and it said:

Dear James,

Your parents tell me that you are taking your final examinations. I hope when this reaches you they will be over, but if not, console yourself with the new knowledge that in his will your grandfather left you (as well as your brothers and sisters) a considerable legacy. My initial estimate is that the amount left each of you (in a mixture of equities and bonds) should total about $38,000 before tax.

I have hastened to write you first because I imagine that your education is now drawing to a close, and I would not want you to make any career decisions without the benefit of knowing of this inheritance.

We all miss your grandfather very much, especially Sundays at the Club. Have you had a chance to go round any of the Scottish courses? I will never forget playing St. Andrews with Art Mesic back in 1960. Highly recommended.

Best wishes,

Ed Weil

Of course I was excited by the news, but I almost immediately sobered at the thought that not all the money in the world was going to let me stay in Oxford if I did badly in my exams. I could thus not afford, in that sense, to celebrate; nor even to allow this astonishing windfall to distract me. For the next few days I wouldn't talk to anyone about this, I decided; for a change, work could come first.

Thirteen

✻ *On Wednesday I* took my seventh paper. Friday morning would see me through the eighth and last. As I sat harnessing my dwindling powers of concentration a minor part of me was cheered by the nearness of the end, my new inheritance, the prospect of seeing Celia again. Mostly, however, I was intent on checking my fatigue before it intervened and cost me success in the exams. For, half-consciously, I knew I was doing well, partly through luck in the questions offered, partly through a kind of quick, cheap eloquence in forming my replies. Most of all because I had not yet panicked, lost my head, surrendered in the face of my incontestable ignorance.

I finished the paper early, running out of things to say about Wittgenstein on silence; I left Schools and started to walk up the High towards college. With a free day before my final paper I felt slightly liberated from the grind, and for the first time I thought at length of the import of Ed Weil's letter. I was not suddenly vastly rich, but I had been given a certain freedom, a latitude to let me do the substantial piece of writing I now knew I wanted to do. I had not discussed the news with anyone, and as I walked down St. Aldates it occurred to me that I should at least telephone home and let my parents know that I had received the letter.

Phoning the States was cumbersome; direct dialing had yet to be introduced. The simplest way was to reverse the charges and place the call through an operator from a pay phone. But in my new-found affluence it seemed a bit mean to freeload off my parents; I decided to pay for the call myself. I didn't want to spend twenty minutes shoving coins through a slot, so I walked past my college down the street towards the International Phone Bureau. It sat on an amorphous spur of the hideous one-way system that consumes the south edge of the city center. I walked into the office, placed my call with the attendant, then sat in one of three open cubicles waiting to be connected. A heavy-set man sat by the phone nearest mine, talking in what he may have taken to be a quiet voice, but its American vigor was distinctly audible to me.

My parents didn't answer, and I decided to call Celia: there was nobody waiting for the phone so the attendant didn't mind placing a London call. As I went back to the cubicle I saw that the man in the one next to mine was Howard Jackson. It was not an unlikely place to encounter him; I nearly tapped him on the shoulder to say hello but decided to spare him the intrusion. When Celia answered I forgot about him.

She was friendly. "I was just thinking about you. You're almost done, aren't you?"

"One more to go. Will I see you after it?"

"Let me see," she said slowly, and my heart sank. "My diary's just here. Oh yes, maybe I can manage it." She laughed lightly. "I'm teasing you. Audrey's driving up and says she'll give me a lift. You're due out at noon, aren't you?"

"That's right. In the High Street."

"I know it," she said. "Tell me, how's it going?"

"Not too bad. I'm a little distracted." And I told her as succinctly as I could about the thirty-eight thousand dollars, although I didn't mention a figure.

"Golly," she said appreciatively. "What good news."

"Not bad. You need a loan?" I said flippantly, thinking of her Courtauld fees.

"Now don't start that again," she said measuredly with some annoyance. "I'm doing very nicely, thank you very much. I've even got the money for my fees saved up now."

I resisted the temptation to ask "from Daddy?" and was suddenly and painfully aware that she could say "Grandpa?" to me and my new *richesse*. She may have sensed this suppressed urge in me, for she added impatiently, "It's *my* money, damn you, I earned it."

"Well, that's more than I can say about my bonanza."

She waited a second as this sank in, as much in me, really, as in her. "Never mind. It's how you use it that counts. But I think you'd better stop gambling. You don't seem especially lucky to me, not if that night at the Connoisseur Club is anything to go by."

"You've got a point. But what should I spend it on?"

"Why feel as if you have to spend it at all? Wait and use it on something important."

"I plan to. Actually, I'm thinking of staying on." She said nothing and I continued, "Staying here. To do another degree. A thesis. What do you think of that?"

"What I think isn't very important, is it? How long have you been considering this?"

"A while," I said and was about to say more when Howard Jackson's voice distracted me. "You promised," he said, not loudly, but with great urgency. "They better stand up or I'm in deep trouble."

"What's that?" I said to Celia, for she had said something I hadn't heard.

"I said I've got to go now. I have a Mr. Ogasawara waiting for me."

I felt an irrational twinge of jealousy. "Who is he?"

She laughed again. It was a wonderful laugh; it felt like a light breeze in a sauna. "One of my chums in the tourist trade."

"I see," I said. I had no right to pry, I knew.

Howard was suddenly talking again. "It's just some kid causing trouble." He paused. "Some English kid." Another pause. "I don't know why."

"He's seventy-three years old," Celia was saying. "Even if I liked older men that would be going it a bit."

"I'll see you Friday then?"

"Yes, don't worry. Worry about your exams."

"There's only one left."

"Well, worry about it then. And don't think about the money. It will only corrupt you."

"I'll think about you instead."

"Silly boy. Goodbye." And before I could return her farewell she had put the phone down. I felt for a moment as if I'd forgotten something, then realized I was privy to another conversation. What Howard Jackson had said suddenly sunk in. Then he continued next to me, saying, "No, no, she doesn't know a thing. For all she knows every page is what it's supposed to be. She's as clean as the driven snow and I want to keep it that way. But just in case this thing falls through I need a back-up buyer. You hear me?"

He stopped to listen to the other end. A woman entered the office and I quickly picked up the receiver in my cubicle to make it seem that I was still talking. Howard said, "If you're right and they hold up then they won't be looking so hard. We'll be home free." After a minute more he said, "We'll be back soon. Count on me coming down in about six weeks. I'll call you Friday. It should all be over then. Bye." As he hung up I turned my back to him and waited a good two minutes to let him get clear away from the office.

I was confused by what I'd overheard. What were supposed to hold up? The Lee papers? The island papers he wanted to sell?

I went over to the cashier. "That man who just left, the American. Was he talking to the States?"

"Yes," the woman said and looked at me. "Why?"

"I think I know him," I said. "Would you know where he'd placed his call?"

"I'm sorry but surely that's his affair."

I smiled widely. "Of course. It's just I wondered if that was Howard Jackson. He knew my Daddy when I was growing up. In New Orleans," I said, pronouncing it like a native.

"Is that how you say it? I thought it sounded funny."

"Thanks," I said. That confirmed it. Since Howard had called New Orleans I'd take three-to-one it was Smiley he'd been talking to. So they were the partners in crime—and Lafayette Jackson an unwitting and innocent accomplice. No wonder I couldn't reconcile the thought of deliberate fraud with the woman: the two just didn't connect.

Fourteen

"In Hegel's political philosophy we can find the seeds that later became the distorted plants of 20th century fascism. To blame the progenitor for the nature of such distant progeny is to credit him with a political vision entirely alien to his time, but Hegel can nonetheless still be criticized for the lack of foresight about the unpleasant implications of his credos. Arguably, Hegel was a myopic German banana."

I kept the last sentence strictly in my head and with the rest of this meaningless conclusion finished my exams early, pocketed my pen, and deposited my script with the invigilator. I walked through the halls of Schools alone, a quarter-hour before anyone else. Try as I could to pad my remarks, I had run out of things to say.

When I emerged from the building the usual crowd was only just beginning to form. I was happy to miss the tumult, the sprays of cheap fizzy wine and the vain battle of the police to restrain the students and keep the High Street traffic flowing. As I left, a shout from my left drew me up the High Street, and I found McCandles and Audrey waving madly at me, both of them jumping up into view over the head of a large bobby. I walked over to them and found

Celia standing there as well. She wore a thin fuchsia cotton dress and looked dazzling in her blonde way. Somehow in a so-so spring she had contrived to get quite tan.

"Congratulations!" all three of them shouted, and I laughed and drank from the bottle McCandles shoved into my hand. It was cheap Italian stuff that tasted like 7-Up.

"I didn't expect Dom Perignon," I said with a grimace, "but this is awful."

"A purely ceremonial libation," said McCandles. "We've reserved the better stuff for dinner."

"Dinner? What about lunch?"

McCandles shook his head. "These two have to go meet Celia's cousin. I thought we'd all have dinner tonight." The two women nodded, said goodbye, and crossed the High Street. I was left standing with McCandles, feeling suddenly deflated.

He seemed unperturbed by my visible disappointment. "Have you got to rush back to college right away? I mean, did you plan to celebrate this afternoon?"

"I thought I was going to celebrate with you guys this afternoon." I was simultaneously baffled and aggrieved. "Don't you remember?"

"I know," said McCandles coolly, "but something's happened."

We were walking up the High, through the growing crowd of students come to greet their colleagues leaving Schools. I stopped and said, "Look, what's going on? If you've got bad news for me I want to know it right away." Either someone in my family had died or McCandles was doing a terrible job of taking me to a surprise party.

"It's Newcastle," McCandles said smoothly.

"What happened?" I asked, remembering that the committee for the new library had met that morning. "Did he present any evidence about the Lee papers?"

"No, he wasn't there. He's in the Warneford."

"What's he got?" I said uncomprehendingly.

"Do you know what the Warneford is?"

"Sure. It's one of the hospitals."

McCandles looked exasperated. "Yes, it's a hospital; it's a *mental* hospital."

"Newcastle is mentally ill?" You have to realize how tired I was; the elation of finishing my exams was giving way to exhaustion.

"Of course he's mentally ill," said McCandles loudly; a passing tourist stared at us. "Come on," he said more quietly, "I've got Audrey's car around the corner. Bicker's in it. We're going to visit him."

"I'm supposed to come along?"

"Sure," he said blithely, as if I were a key reason for Newcastle's stay in the Warneford. "You've got to help me calm Newcastle down."

"Have you talked to him yet?"

"Not yet. He left a message with the porter at Christ Church. They must have allowed him one phone call."

"Hello, Charlie," I said to Bicker as we arrived at the car. He had finished his exams the day before but seemed less than exuberant. He stayed in the back seat and McCandles drove as we inched through the mob of students now besieging Schools. I took off my gown and undid my tie.

"Turn right at the bottom of Headington Hill," said Bicker as we passed the scaffolding that enveloped the front of Magdalen. I had yet to see Magdalen Tower without this protective garb of pipe.

"Have you already been to see Newcastle?" I asked Bicker.

"No, but one of the Magdalen kids cracked up last year and I went to the Warneford to see him."

"Charlie's an old hand at mental cases," McCandles said sarcastically.

I ignored him. "When did Newcastle go in?"

"This morning," said McCandles. "I went to this ridiculous meeting in Balliol about the American Studies Library. It was full of Anglophile Americans. You know, James, the kind you liked so much at Yale. Harris tweeds and English shoes. I sat through the whole thing with these horrible people waiting for Newcastle to show up and make his speech. I think Hubert must have known he wasn't coming. Anyway, the Jacksons were there; they looked happy as clams. It looks certain that the library will go ahead now. That means the fund will buy the papers about the island from Lafayette. Once Newcastle didn't show up everything went lickety-split."

"I had a drink with him the night before last," Bicker interjected. "He seemed okay then. Nothing he said indicated he wouldn't show up this morning."

"Wait a minute," said McCandles, raising a hand from the steering wheel. "You haven't heard the rest of it. An hour ago I ran into the Senior Tutor at college. He told me Newcastle was caught breaking into Rhodes House Library at three o'clock last night. When they found him he assaulted one of the Bulldogs. The police came and wanted to throw him in jail, but the Dean of Christ Church persuaded them to stick him in the Warneford."

McCandles went on in jauntier fashion. "Maybe Newcastle will like the Warneford; a stay there may do him some good. From what I understand, the place is almost a resort. Good food, plenty of rest, beautiful surroundings. My aunt, you know, the one who wanted to adopt a boat child, used to spend her annual vacation in the loony bin. 'My special two weeks off,' she used to say. She wasn't any more crackers than Newcastle is."

The Warneford turned out to be next to the golf course, where I had played several pleasant, solitary rounds the summer before. We had difficulty finding Newcastle, for the hospital consisted of bungalow-like structures linked by long corridors that splayed out like the arms of a molecular model. Finally a nurse spotted us wandering around and directed us to Newcastle's room. He was the sole occupant of a "semi-private," with a view of the grounds and, further away, the 18th hole. The walls of his room were painted a bright yellow, something I found startling since I had once been told that yellow is the color most often associated with madness. The floor was dark linoleum, but half of it was lit up by a wide fan of sunlight that poured through the enormous windows. During our visit, the sun strayed in and out of clouds, so the light in the room would alter suddenly, from the gloomiest gray to sudden illumination. I noticed there were no locks or mesh windows. Apparently, Newcastle was not thought dangerous, despite his assault on a Bulldog the night before.

He sat, wearing a dingy bathrobe, in a chintz armchair by the window. His bed was covered with books and papers and on his lap he held a book which he was reading intently even after our tentative knock on his open door. At last looking up, he did not seem displeased to see us, although his first words were hardly friendly. "You can't stay long," he announced briskly. "They're very strict here."

"That's all right," McCandles said tactfully. He acted far more at home than either Bicker or I. "James here has just finished Schools, so he's dog-tired. We won't stay long. How are you?"

"Better, thank you," he said crisply. "I've kept the annoyances down to a minimum. At first, the nurses wouldn't leave me alone. I told them I had work to do, but they didn't take me seriously."

"Have you got everything you need?" Bicker asked nervously. "Do you want any books or magazines?"

With a flourish, Newcastle pointed to his bed, which was covered in books and papers. "I have more than enough to keep me busy, thank you."

"You have a nice view," I said, more for something to say than out of any deep conviction. There was an old woman in khaki shorts on the 18th green.

"I find the view distracting. But at least I'm alone here," Newcastle said, motioning with his head toward the other, empty bed.

There was an awkward silence which Bicker ended by saying feebly, "I see you've got a television."

"I only watch the news. Somoza's gone," he said with a nod. "Just as we predicted. No thanks to Lafayette Jackson."

The mention of this name seemed to lift the veil from our polite, innocuous queries. Our curiosity grew too great and Bicker finally blurted out, "Newcastle, what happened? Why are you here?"

Newcastle sighed and closed his book. "It was a disastrous oversight on my part. I took this all too literally." He tapped the book significantly with his fingers and I saw that it was again *An Enquiry* by Carter and Pollard.

"What is he talking about?" asked Bicker, reflecting my own confusion.

"Carter and Pollard," McCandles said patiently, almost pedagogically, "were two bibliographical scholars who exposed a large number of fraudulent first editions created and disseminated by T. J. Wise, then the most eminent bibliographer in the world. The case they compiled against Wise was devastating and irrefutable, and it's all set forth in *An Enquiry*. Yet in it they're careful never to state directly that Wise was the architect of the fraud; they just let all the evidence point his way."

"When was this?" I asked, wondering how it could have helped Newcastle's researches into the Lee papers.

"In the thirties. Wise had been famous for many years; his downfall came at the end of his life. However, the important thing wasn't so much *what* Carter and Pollard showed were fakes as *how* they did it. They used what were for the time revolutionary techniques to prove the fraud. Paper analysis, typeface analysis, examination of printers' fonts—ask me sometime to tell you the tale of the kernless j. The two of them applied scientific techniques to what was traditionally the province of the amateur. They received a certain amount of flak for it; it seemed to some a bit too redolent of, shall we say, 'an undesirable professionalism'? And both Carter and Pollard were very young then. They were actually awfully brave to attack an established figure like Wise."

"Me, too," said Newcastle from his bed. "I'm brave attacking this woman. Don't you think?"

There was an embarrassed silence that I eventually broke. "Well, what did you take too literally then?" I asked Newcastle.

Newcastle quickly opened the book and found the pertinent page. He said loudly, "This is quoted by Carter and Pollard from the News Bulletin of the Paper Section of the National Bureau of Standards . . . 'Rag fibers were found exclusively until 1867, when the first straw fibers were found, followed by ground wood in 1869 and chemical wood in 1870'. In the U.S., Carter and Pollard also say, 'Esparto was not introduced into their paper-mills until 1907'."

I looked at Bicker; Bicker looked at me. It was clear to us both that Newcastle really was off his head. But McCandles, bibliophile McCandles, the sly McCandles who knew Carter and Pollard backwards and forwards, grew visibly excited. "And?" he said to Newcastle leadingly.

"Well it's perfectly obvious, isn't it?" said Newcastle.

"What is?" I almost shouted, infuriated that McCandles was nodding vigorously in agreement.

"Look on the bed," said Newcastle wearily, and I went over to the papers strewn over the rumpled covers. "Pick up the small envelope and look at what's inside."

"Be careful," warned McCandles.

"Why should he be?" Newcastle said. "The bloody thing's probably less than five years old."

Inside the envelope I found a faded piece of thick, yellowing paper. Attached to it by a paper clip was a white slip with typewriting on it. I slowly drew both out and read the slip aloud: "Letter from Robert E. Lee to Jefferson Davis, 2 July 1863." Bicker came and looked over my shoulder as I read the letter aloud:

2 July 1863

Sir,

A resolution will soon be upon us. Pray God it is in our favor. I am striving to insure that this be so.

yr hble servt,

R Lee

"An obvious fake," Newcastle declared. "Lee never wrote like that, and certainly not to Jefferson Davis. As if the day before Pickett's charge he'd waste time scribbling a note that would take three days to reach Richmond. Besides which, he had terrible diarrhea that day. And look at the condition of the thing—why, it's almost pristine."

"Mint," said McCandles pedantically. "Fine or near-fine at any rate."

"Newcastle," I said impatiently, "where did you get this from?"

"Rhodes House. There's lots more where that came from."

"That's where the Lee papers are being stored," McCandles explained. "Until they build this new library."

"Did you take this last night?" I asked Newcastle.

"Goodness, no. I took it away weeks ago. Last night I was trying to *return* it. Do you have any idea how much noise breaking a single pane of glass makes?"

"Why were you there at three in the morning? Why not during the day?"

"They've denied me all further access to the papers. The librarian took against me from the start. A fascist, of course. Hubert must have said something to him because one day he simply said the papers were closed to me. 'Should you wish to appeal the decision you may speak to the Keeper of Western Manuscripts in Bodley.' The total shit. But you see, I had to get the letter back. Once they'd discovered it missing they'd have come straight for me." He said this as if aggrieved to be the object of such suspicion, as if he hadn't taken the letter from Rhodes House after all.

"How would they know it was you?"

"I've spent more time looking at the letters in the last six months than anyone else. Oxford's not exactly crawling with American Civil War buffs. And as I told you, Hubert's already suspicious of my interest in them. They've nothing to do with my thesis, you know."

"But why did you take the letter away if you'd already seen it?" Bicker asked.

"Because I had to prove it was a fake. And it is a fake."

"Only you can't prove it?"

"If I had more time I could," said Newcastle plaintively.

"But how was this," I said, meaning the letter, "supposed to prove it?"

"The paper," McCandles said emphatically.

I thought I caught their drift. "Paper analysis? When it was made?"

"Exactly," said Newcastle. "The letter's so obviously bogus that I assumed it was of very recent vintage—only Smiley in New Orleans knows just how recent—and that it was written on recent stock jimmied up to look old. Virtually any 20th century paper will have acid in it—or esparto grass. Since these kinds of paper were first introduced into the States only well *after* the Civil War, then if the Lee letter contained any of either, it was a *prima facie* fraud. So I took the letter away and sent it to specialists in London. Look at the letter on my bed."

I soon found a typed letter from D. Hunnicot & Sons, Graphologists, Ink, and Paper Specialists, Camberwell Green, London.

> Dear Mr. Newcastle:
>
> We are pleased to inform you that tests we have applied to the document in question were uniformly negative. No traces of acid, grass, or straw content were discerned in any of the sample.
>
> Thus you may rest assured that as far as the material composition of the document is concerned there is no reason to doubt its provenance.
>
> We trust you will find these results satisfactory. We take pleasure in enclosing an invoice for £79.66 and will be happy to be of service in future.

"But they say they're *not* fakes," I declared.

"Hardly," said Newcastle scornfully. "They simply say the paper *could* date from the Civil War."

"It was an expensive way to find out," I said, examining the bill.

"Worth every penny if it had let me expose that woman."

"They seem to think you wanted to defend the letter's authenticity," I said, putting it back on the bed.

"I wasn't very well going to tell Hunnicot & Sons what I was looking for. They might have leaked it to the press." I heard McCandles give a small groan. "In any event, there's not a trace of acid, or anything but rag in the paper. It could, conceivably, date from 1863, though I'd give a pound to a penny that it's post-Second World War."

"So you couldn't testify," I said.

Newcastle didn't answer for a moment. "No," he said quietly. "I couldn't. I didn't have anything concrete to show."

"Maybe the papers aren't fake," Bicker said carefully. "And maybe Lafayette Jackson, I mean I know she's no good, but maybe her island stuff—*those* papers—are real, too. It doesn't make her any better," he said soothingly to Newcastle, "but it's just possible they're the real thing."

"No," I said, sharply enough to make all three look at me in surprise, for I suddenly saw exactly what had happened. But I also realized almost immediately that my new knowledge wasn't going to help Newcastle; it would only serve to depress him further, possibly even prolong his stay in the Warneford. So I regretted my outburst and said weakly now, "I'm just certain the papers are no good," without further explanation.

The surprised looks on their faces subsided to uninterest. "Well," asked McCandles, "what's to be done?"

Newcastle shrugged. After recounting the history of his failed investigations, he seemed despondent. "Presumably they'll have to let me out of here at some point. I wonder if I'll be charged with burglary. Probably the university won't allow it." He added bitterly, "Instead, they'll hang me in their own way. They'll soon find out the letter's missing and then blame me for that. They'll send me down as soon as is inhumanly possible."

At first there seemed nothing at all to say to this, but then I had an inspiration. Newcastle had not managed to expose Lafayette Jackson and I had no interest in doing so myself—not when I knew it was her husband who was the crook. But it might be possible to save Newcastle from complete disgrace without further harassment of the hapless woman. "Wait a minute," I announced, and they looked at me again, somewhat skeptically given my unsupported outburst of before. "*We'll* put the letter back in Rhodes House for you."

"What?" said McCandles incredulously.

"Why not? They won't let him in, but they'll let us."

"I doubt it," said Newcastle. "Not after last night. I'm sure they won't let anyone near them now."

"We'll see," I said, collecting the letter from his bed. "Come on," I told McCandles and Bicker, "we have work to do."

Once outside, in the spring air of sanity, I began to consider what I'd done. McCandles, catching up to me by the car, reinforced my more sober appraisal.

"Are you crazy, too?" he demanded as we drove off. "What do you think you're doing? If Newcastle wants to indulge in an extended bout of self-destruction, well and fine—it's not exactly unexpected. But why drag yourself into it?"

"Don't you see?" I said to both McCandles and Bicker. "He picked the wrong ones."

"Who picked what wrong ones?"

"The wrong papers. He checked the Lee papers. They're fine—at least nothing is wrong with them that Newcastle can prove. It's the *island* papers that are phony. Newcastle should have tried to have them examined."

"How do you know this?" asked McCandles.

"Howard Jackson."

"He told you?" McCandles asked doubtfully. "Just like that."

"No, no," I said quickly, and then I told them about overhearing Howard Jackson on the phone. "But I didn't really get it then," I concluded. "It took until now for me to figure out just what Howard meant—'*If they hold up then they won't be looking so hard. We'll be home free.*' At the time I didn't understand it. But I do now. He meant that if the Lee papers stood up to scrutiny—remember, Newcastle had been telling everyone he would prove they were fakes—then the island papers wouldn't even be looked at very closely."

I paused to reflect for a moment. "And he's right. Nothing can touch him now. Not with Newcastle in the nuthouse and almost in jail. No one will listen to him ever again. The University's already been embarrassed by the cloud Newcastle managed to put over the Jacksons. Now that it's passed they won't let anyone move it back there again. The only thing we can do is try to save Newcastle from real trouble when they discover the paper's missing."

Bicker did not share my equanimity. "Shit. So she did fake the papers. And she's going to get away with it."

"She didn't fake the papers. Howard did. And Smiley, the bookseller. From what Howard said, Lafayette doesn't know anything about it. Which doesn't surprise me."

"Bullshit. She must know," said Bicker. "I don't believe you heard him right."

"Charlie, all you ever believe are your own preconceptions."

"Relax you two," McCandles commanded. "Don't take it all so seriously. But tell me, James," he said, his tone softening, "just how do you think you'll get this letter back in there?"

"I'll be goddamned if I know," I said, fingering the envelope in my jacket pocket. "Got any ideas?"

McCandles' face brightened. "Dozens. It calls for an inspired imagination that you patently lack. I can't let you get caught and end up in the Warneford, too."

"What does that mean?" I asked hopefully.

"It means I'll drop you off as soon as we can get Bicker out of this car and then I'll meet you in half an hour, once you've changed your clothes. Rhodes House Library's open until five-thirty today, so we'll have plenty of time. But what about you, Charlie?" he said, addressing the back seat. "Are you game?"

Bicker said nothing for a moment and McCandles added caustically, "Or are you worried about what your constituents might say?"

"Fuck you," said Bicker, climbing out of the car. "I'll see you both at Blackwell's in thirty minutes."

"Charlie's feeling guilty," said McCandles as we drove up the High. "He'd never admit as much, but I'm quite certain he feels he egged Newcastle on."

"Maybe he did. Maybe we all did."

"Oh come on," said McCandles, slowing down to let me out. "Newcastle's impervious to external influence. Don't go all analytic on me just when things are getting interesting. You've got a front row center seat. Why give it up now?"

I went back to my room and changed into a preppy journalist's uniform of blue blazer, Brooks Brothers tie, gray slacks, and loafers. As I carefully put the letter in my jacket pocket I did not feel tense so much as exhilarated; goddamn McCandles, I thought wistfully, just when I thought I'd put away childish things.

The three of us met outside Blackwell's and walked in conspiratorial silence towards Rhodes House. Outside the King's Arms recent finalists like me sat in the sun wearing their gowns and drinking pints of beer. Empty bottles of fizzy wine littered the pavement.

We found the librarian in his office. As we knocked and entered, McCandles whispered, "Leave this to me." The librarian, a man named Carillon, was sitting at his desk, reading a magazine called *Dry Fly Fishing* and munching on a chocolate biscuit. He was a gross, florid man, dressed in oversized county tweeds with orange Ducker shoes. He wore a thin gold chain pocket watch on a fob, which he peered at ostentatiously as we entered.

"My name is McCandles," said the one and the same, and Carillon nodded in vague recognition at this regular user of his library. McCandles continued in a meekly petitioning voice. "I was wondering if it might be possible to look briefly at the Robert E. Lee papers."

"Closed to students for the indefinite future," the librarian said without looking up.

Instantly, McCandles' tone changed, assuming a sudden tenor of authority. "This," he said, turning to Bicker, "is Senator Charles Bicker from New Hampshire. And this gentleman," he said turning to me, "is a representative of the press. From *Time* magazine in New York."

Carillon now paid rather more attention to us and stood up. I moved forward to introduce myself and shake his hand, and Bicker did the same. Carillon seemed a little stunned by this aggressive pressing of the flesh and it was clear we now had him on the defensive. Certainly Bicker looked the part, I thought, until I noticed his shirt was badly frayed and his shoes—well, his shoes might reasonably be called boating shoes if you were speaking of a second-rate dinghy.

Fortunately, Carillon seemed sufficiently impressed by our importance not to inspect our attire very closely. McCandles continued, speaking with the impersonal deliberation of a guide: "Senator Bicker is an alumnus of this university, an old Oxonian, a Magdalen man and a Rhodes Scholar. He particularly wanted to revisit Rhodes House and indeed the

Warden has recently suggested that he have a look at the library. The Warden also mentioned that the Robert E. Lee papers are being stored here until completion of the new library. That's why I ask if it would be possible for the Senator to have a look at them."

This rapid-fire palaver, tissue of lies, collage of taradiddle, fiction, and downright whoppers, worked. "That should be possible," Carillon said with false cheerfulness. He looked straight but not suspiciously at us and said, "As a matter of fact, there's a representative of the press looking at them at this very moment."

"Who is he?" I asked nervously.

"He? She, you mean," said the librarian. "A lady from *Newsweek*. One of your rivals, I imagine."

Christ! I thought, how was I going to carry this off? What would I say when this rival started asking questions? I didn't even know the name of *Time*'s editor. McCandles tried to come to my rescue. "If someone's already there," he said to Carillon, "there's no need to trouble you to accompany us. I've been in the archive room before, I know where the papers are."

"It's no trouble at all," said Carillon. "I'll be happy to escort you upstairs."

McCandles again demurred; Carillon again insisted. Further resistance on our part to his chaperonage would only arouse suspicion; it seemed our bluff would soon be called.

And then providence materialized in the form of a telephone call. An abrupt, trilling scream came from beneath *Dry Fly Fishing* and Carillon first looked startled, then hesitated, and finally picked up the shrill instrument. "Rhodes House Library," he barked. "Hello," he paused, "hello. Yes, yes it is. Where? San Francisco. Ah yes, hello Professor."

"We'll just have a look at the Reading Room," said McCandles, making reassuring hand signals to the librarian. Before

he could disengage himself from his trans-Atlantic conversation, we were out the door and moving rapidly up the stairs
to the room where, McCandles declared, the papers were
confined.

As we ascended, Bicker said tersely to me, "You've got to
get rid of this woman."

"How the hell am I going to do that?"

"Who knows?" said McCandles. "Think of something,
and quick. It's your turn to pull a rabbit out of the hat."

As we opened the door to the archive room, an oily smell
of leather and ambition assaulted us. Standing against the
center table (a long refectory table of dark oak), wearing
brown boots and a suit of burgundy velvet, staring down at
an immense folio ledger book open on the table, was the
redoubtable Sally Archimedes, B.A. Princeton, Rhodes Scholar, and aspiring member of the working press.

"Hi boys," she said with much the same impatience Newcastle showed when interrupted. "I can't visit with you now.
I'm working."

"For whom?" asked McCandles.

"For *Newsweek*," she said proudly, staring at me. She was
fiercely competitive in her journalistic ambitions and never
knew quite whether to regard me as a threat—the political
magazines I wrote for had the unimpressive habit of folding
soon after my appearance in their pages.

"What are you working on?" Bicker asked, knowing full
well.

"I'm not sure," said Sally with a baffled tone, looking down
at the folio before her. I say folio, because it was roughly that
size, but in fact the volume was something of a scrapbook,
with double-sided clear plastic pages holding the documents.

She looked keen to say more, but fear of losing her scoop
restrained her—she might not find the scoop but she'd be
damned if she gave it to somebody else.

"Relax," I said. "Bicker and I are just following McCandles around. He thinks he left his briefcase in here. That's all we're doing."

"Well, it isn't in here," she said firmly.

"Come on, Sally," McCandles said coaxingly. "Let us in on the big secret." He gave her a playful poke in the ribs and she giggled slightly, seemingly against her will. "Do let me assist you my dear," McCandles said in a Robert Morley voice, and Sally giggled again. Her short thick frame contracted and expanded under its burgundy cover as she struggled not to laugh out loud. "I am a professionally-trained student of history," McCandles went on with mock-pomposity, "there is surely some role I may play in your investigations."

"It's these goddamned papers," Sally declared. "Your pal Newcastle told me they were fakes. What a story that would make," she said, eyeing me nervously. "According to Newcastle they're obviously phony. But I don't see anything wrong with them at all."

Poor Sally, I thought, what did she expect—a give-away deceit-colored stain running through the pages, a resonating hum buried within each document that said FAKE in a dog whistle-type tone audible only to stringers for *Newsweek*?

McCandles must have had the same thoughts, although perhaps less charitably conceived. "For fuck's sake, Sally," he said curtly, playing to her addiction to foul-mouthed talk, "how the hell are *you* going to tell they're phony? They've already fooled several professional historians. Give up the ghost, now, and come with us. Cantucci's throwing a party and there's supposed to be champagne."

But Sally stayed fast, convinced of her unique powers of discernment. "No thanks. You guys go ahead, maybe I'll show up later. I want to look at these some more."

McCandles rolled his eyes at me. If we didn't get her out of there soon, Carillon would appear and our chance of replacing the letter would be gone. "Sally," I said as persuasively as possible, "Tuchins is going to be at the party. He's doing a piece for the States on Bright Young Things. I'm sure he'll expect to see you there."

This set her back. Tuchins, an American political correspondent based in London, was something of a mentor for young Sally. He had fallen for her, in fact, while writing a story on the first women Rhodes Scholars. It was not, I think, a sexual infatuation, despite his considerable reputation for philandering. Instead, Tuchins treated her avuncularly, taking her along on stories, letting her stay in his spare room in Kensington, getting her some plum assignments. Tuchins once told a New York journalist I knew that he'd "adopted" Sally. Whatever their precise relationship, it had proven an invaluable connection for her, and if I and others were wont to make fun of it, I knew that for me at least envy helped inspire this mockery—especially since I was usually writing for political journals with a combined circulation of four.

"He didn't say anything to me about coming to Oxford. I saw him last Friday, too. I'm sure he would have told me."

"It's sudden," I said. "Cantucci heard about this article somehow, and you know what a self-promoter he is. He rang up Tuchins this morning and persuaded him to come. If you don't tell Tuchins, he'll think Cantucci really *is* a Bright Young Thing. Can you see that on the AP wire back home?"

This seemed to be the clincher; Sally bristled and closed the folio. "Let's go," she said, heading for the door, "I'm not letting that creep get away with it."

Bicker and McCandles walked out with her and I surreptitiously lingered. Quickly I looked down at the enormous ledger. Fortunately, it was divided into sections, marked clearly by tabs attached to the outer edges of the plastic pages. One was marked LEE/DAVIS and I lifted the heavy pages carefully until I came to that section. Sure enough, there were letters from Lee to Davis, carefully inserted, and I soon saw they were ordered chronologically: 1861, 1862, 1863—January, March, June, July—July 2! There was a label—REL-JD 2 July 1863—and a blank sheet of plastic. I took the absent document from my pocket, unfolded it and carefully laid it down between the thin film of plastic. Then I closed the ledger book and walked out of the room. I found my friends waiting for me on the landing below, along with Sally. "What's the hold-up?" asked Bicker querulously to allay Sally's suspicions.

"Sorry," I said vaguely, "I was just looking around. I've never been in that place before."

As we reached the landing Carillon emerged from his office. "Gentlemen, I am so sorry. One of your countrymen on the telephone, rather a loquacious gentleman. Do let me show you the papers."

"Actually," said McCandles, "I'm afraid we haven't the time now. The Senator," he said, ignoring Sally's wondering stare, "was due at Balliol ten minutes ago. Perhaps we can come back tomorrow."

"Oh dear," the librarian said guiltily. "It's my fault for talking so long on the phone. Are you quite sure you can't look briefly at the papers now?"

"Quite certain, I'm afraid," said Bicker. "Thank you anyway. I've very much enjoyed the opportunity to look round the library. It's most impressive."

"Well, again my apologies. Do come back if you have time. The Lee papers are well worth viewing." He turned and went back to his office while we continued down the stairs. Suddenly, Sally stopped and clutched a carved Zimbabwe bird on the newel post. "What did he say? What did that fat man just say?"

"Nothing, Sally. Let's go to the party." I tried to put my arm through hers, but she was having none of it.

"Let go of me, you bastard. You lied to me, you came here to see the same papers. There *is* something wrong with them." She looked accusingly at me, her heavy jaw clenched with anger. "You son of a bitch, if you steal my story, I'll make sure you never work in journalism again." And pushing past me and Bicker ("Senator," she hissed), she marched back up the stairs.

Slightly subdued by this outburst, we walked out the door onto the Rhodes House back lawn. The daffodils were in full bloom and McCandles suddenly swooped down, picked one, and stuck it sideways through his teeth. Dancing across the turf he extracted the flower, shouting, "You'll never work in journalism again. Gone the chance of dinner with Ben Bradlee, gone the by-line's resonant appeal, gone the copy-editor's sweet smile as he turns your copy back to you, perfect as buttermilk on a pig-smelling day. Gone, gone, gone! And all for the sake of the purloined letter." He stopped short and laughed again. "But just think of fat Sally. She could sit up there for a year and a half, looking for her scoop, and never find a goddamned thing, now that you've put the letter back."

"What letter?" I said blankly.

It was nice to watch McCandles lose his cool for a change. "Just kidding," I said when his jaw had dropped sufficiently.

Fifteen

I slept soundly the rest of the afternoon. Waking around six I showered and put on my preppy ensemble again, then left for Christ Church and McCandles' room. The chapel quad of my college was deserted except for Michael Shambling, passed out on a bench. He had had no fun at all that I could recall for two years, and I hoped for his sake that he got a First. When I stopped to check my mail box, I heard my name called from the Porter's Lodge. Turning around I saw Emily, my scout, sitting at the switchboard.

"You're finished then?" she inquired in a thick voice. Someone had given her a bottle of hock; it was half-empty.

"All done. Why are you sitting there? Where's the porter?"

"Jinx? He's ill—he's not feeling well at all. Some of the boys took him to the pub at lunch. A terrible thing to do to a man."

I could discern no irony in her words. "Is that what they're trying to do to you?" I asked, nodding towards the wine bottle.

"Oh no. Indeed no. I like a small glass with my supper. It's like medicine." She paused. "I like you Americans," she said dreamily. "Bourbon. Bourbon whiskey," she said with a deep, affectionate lilt. And her head fell onto her open palm, then slipped slowly on the desk, unconscious. She was stinko.

In Christ Church others fresh from Schools lingered by the fountain in Tom Quad, still drinking noisily from heavy green bottles. They looked happy and relaxed, with that special casual arrogance Christ Church seems to impart. They were the focus of so much English hatred, but to me they all appeared, in their complete ease, like nephews of Lord Peter Wimsey.

I found McCandles' door ajar and after knocking walked right in. Celia was in one of his chairs, wearing gray corduroys and boots with a blue blouse and paisley scarf. The effect was deliberately informal.

"Hello," I said, "where's Wilmarth and Audrey?"

"They've gone off to a pub. We're supposed to meet them at the restaurant."

"You didn't go with them?"

"Someone had to wait for you," she said coyly.

"Are we meant to join them at the pub?"

Celia hesitated. "If you want."

"I'd rather drink here," I said, looking at McCandles' bottle of gin.

"Me too," she said, so I mixed us each a warm gin-and-tonic and sat down in the chair across from her.

"You're finished," she said, raising her glass. "Well done."

"Thank God it's over. So tell me about the Japanese."

We were an hour late for the restaurant but McCandles didn't seem to care. He had bought a magnum of champagne at vast expense and our lateness had allowed him to drink most of it. Audrey seemed a little put out about our delayed arrival; I sensed her disapproval of my obvious attraction to Celia. I enjoyed my dinner nonetheless, and afterwards we walked slowly through Cornmarket towards our colleges. I went ahead with Celia, showing her the commercial sights.

"That's Woolworth's," I declared.

"I know," she said. "They tore down the Clarendon Hotel to build it. Tell me, do they save old buildings much in the States?"

"Not much. But I think we do build better modern ones."

"I'm sure you do. Ours are mostly ghastly. If there's a strength in British architecture today it's in renovation, not in making new buildings."

"You won't be very popular with architects for saying that."

"Perhaps, but it's perfectly true. What I like may seem derivative to a megalomaniac designer, but I think it makes life more pleasant for the public."

"I can see that. But it's not a view Americans are used to."

"Give it time," she said with a laugh. We passed a policeman at the top of the High Street. There was no traffic and few people about; voices carried from well down the High. "Aren't you going to show me where you live?" Celia asked.

"Sure. My room's almost as old as Woolworth's."

We turned back to McCandles and Audrey and explained where we were going. "Don't be long," Audrey said to Celia like a mother-hen. "They close the Christ Church gate at midnight."

It was already a quarter past eleven; I said nothing. "Don't worry," said Celia to Audrey, "I can always climb the wall."

She and I turned towards my college, walking in silence. At the Porter's Lodge I noticed Emily was gone. Jinx sat stolidly in her place.

"James." It was Krattenstein, coming from the graduate common room. I introduced him to Celia. He shook her hand quickly and said to me, "Have you heard about your friend Newcastle?"

"I've told you he's not my friend. But yes, I've heard; I've even been to see him in the Warneford."

"Lidodes is fit to be tied."

"Why? He's not the one in the Warneford."

Krattenstein shook his head. "That's not the point. Lidodes is a Proctor this year."

"Oh, Christ," I said reflexively. There were two Proctors in the university each year and they decided the fate of student offenders.

"I wouldn't expect much leniency there; Lidodes is intent on sending him down."

"How unfair."

"This wasn't just a high-spirited prank."

Of course, I knew just what Newcastle's intent had been, but it wouldn't make any differences to Lidodes. Our efforts—those of McCandles, Bicker, and me—were going to prove fruitless through the unhappy coincidence that the one don most antipathetic to Newcastle was in the position of helping set the punishment.

I said, "People have done worse things without being expelled."

"This is a straightforward case of breaking and entering."

"Doubtless Lidodes will see it that way, too," I said, moving towards the quad with Celia. "Thanks for letting me know."

In Chapel Quad the sky was only just shifting from dusk to dark. There was a low moon above the Fellows Garden peeking out behind fat puffs of cloud. "What was that about?" asked Celia.

"You mean the guy back there?"

"Yes. And about your friend. The one they'll send down."

"He's not a friend," I said yet again. "To tell you the truth, I can't stand him. But he's about to get punished for acting on a conviction that I happen to know is correct. The problem is he can't prove it. Nobody can now."

"I think you'd better tell me all about it."

"That will take a while," I said, thinking of how soon Christ Church would be closed.

"I've got all the time in the world," she said calmly, "provided you have something to drink in your room."

So we went there, and I explained the whole ball of wax, the history of Newcastle's obsession with Lafayette Jackson, his hounding of her in print and in person, his finds, his failures, the damning phone call of Howard Jackson I'd over-heard, Lafayette's innocence, everything in fact until it was two-thirty in the morning and we had drunk a liter bottle of red wine in my room.

"How extraordinary," said Celia when I was all through.

"Yes," I said, "that's exactly what it is."

"One wouldn't expect it," she mused, "not at Oxford, anyway."

"It's not the kind of drama I'd associate with this place."

"That's what makes it sad. If you change the particulars, this sort of thing could happen anywhere. But it seems an awful waste of time to do it here. Look what it's done for Newcastle: he's gone and lost his chance forever. He can always play silly buggers wherever he goes, hounding people and so forth, but he won't ever be a proper don, will he, if they send him down?"

"No, he won't. I thought our escapade this afternoon at Rhodes House might have saved him. But you heard Kratten-stein. Lidodes is going to make sure Newcastle gets sent down."

"Even though Newcastle is right about the island papers?"

"Yes. As far as Lidodes knows, Newcastle *wasn't* right, because he hasn't proved anything about the Robert E. Lee papers. I know Lafayette's island evidence is fraudulent, but only because I overheard Howard. That's not evidence; I can't say anything about it."

"Why not? You're not a priest, you know. It's not as if you're a Jesuit who's just listened to a murderer's confession and don't know what to do. This isn't *that* dramatic."

"What do you mean? Why should I do anything to hurt

Lafayette Jackson? Even she doesn't know the papers are fake. Whom would it help to expose her work?"

"Newcastle for one. He may be completely round the twist but he's obviously a real scholar in his own way. Surely he deserves better than what you say he'll get."

"He'll probably get thrown out regardless of what happens to Lafayette Jackson."

"Perhaps. But you'll have done your best for him. And do you really want to see the university buy these papers when you know they're fakes?"

"But Lidodes doesn't know that."

"But *you* do. And you should act on it."

"I still don't see why."

"Because it's right. You can't judge everything by what its consequences may turn out to be: it may hurt Lafayette Jackson, it may not, you don't like Newcastle so you won't do this, and so on. Only adolescents work that way; they can't separate their personal feelings from any objective conclusion. You can."

"And how am I supposed to do this separating?"

"Go see this man Lidodes. He may be perfectly dreadful but he's the only one who can see that Newcastle gets a fair shake. And keep the university from buying these island papers. I'd tell Lidodes what you overheard." She saw my skeptical look and added, "Give me one good reason why you shouldn't go and see him, except that he may not believe you."

"I told you. It might hurt Lafayette Jackson. And she didn't commit the fraud."

"But she profited from it. That's wrong. Her ignorance doesn't mean that her sources are any less tainted; from what you've told me this book of hers relies tremendously on these very letters you know are fake."

"But why is that any business of mine? I'm not even an historian."

"Because you should be telling the truth. Hurting her is not your motive here; you shouldn't let your dislike of Newcastle and your sympathy for Lafayette Jackson keep you from doing what's right."

She stood up and I momentarily thought she was leaving. "Come on," she said casually, "help me put this mattress on the floor. Otherwise there's no way it will hold us both."

And minutes later as she unbuttoned her blue blouse, I said gently, "I'm glad you stayed."

"Go and see Lidodes in the morning," she said severely. Then, lying down beside me, she giggled. "And I'll go and see Audrey. How she won't approve of this!"

Lidodes had two rooms in college: one, a large, high-ceiling chamber with a long mahogany table at which he sat and taught; the other, a small anteroom for visitors that struck me as resembling a dentist's waiting room. There were even copies of *Punch* on a small coffee table.

He kept me waiting in this smaller room for a quarter of an hour, although no one was with him when I first knocked. I sat a little nervously and listened as odd noises came from the adjacent chamber: *whack, whack*—erratic hitting sounds which made me wonder if Lidodes proposed to cane me. When at last he called me in, I looked rapidly around for the source of the noise. Only as I sat did I notice a ruler lying on the table and several of its victims lined neatly on the far edge. Lidodes, I realized, had spent the last quarter-hour killing flies.

"What do you want?" he said with his usual cordiality.

"I want to talk to you about a student who's in trouble. Newcastle."

"Why?"

"I understand you're one of the Proctors this year, so I thought you'd be in a position to influence what happens to him."

"And therefore you hope to influence me? Is this what Americans call 'log-rolling'? How peculiar. I hardly know you. You are a student in this college, where I am a Fellow; you are taught by colleagues of mine. I have encountered you on five, possibly six occasions of brief duration and had only one extended and most unpleasant conversation with you. I know nothing about you, really, except the general opinion that you are moderately intelligent but very, very idle. And, of course, you are an American, which usually seems to mean that I will be addressed by my Christian name by someone half my age and will now be importuned as if I were an elected public official. Given this, I am certain that I cannot help you. Do you still wish to speak to me?"

Not at all, I thought to myself, regretting listening to Celia's suggestion. "Yes," I said, "I learn so much from our conversations."

"I see," he said in the same spirit. "Well, get on with it. What do you have to say?"

"The papers Lafayette Jackson and her husband want to sell the university are fakes. I don't know about the Lee papers; they come from the same source but may well be authentic. Certainly Newcastle can't prove they're fake, though that was the purpose of his breaking into Rhodes House. But the essence of what Newcastle has said about this woman's work is correct. Her book is based on letters that are fake."

"How can you say that? In this whole sordid sequence of accusations, not one firm piece of evidence has yet emerged. What can you show me, please? Show me some evidence."

"I've got nothing to show. But I do have something to tell." And as factually as I could, I related the overheard conversation of Howard Jackson. I explained, too, that because Newcastle's accusations about the Lee papers had gone unproven there would now be no effective opposition to the purchase of the island letters.

"That's evidence?" Lidodes said scornfully when I had

finished. "Innuendo, perhaps. Malicious gossip. Libellous fancy. But evidence? You must be joking. But as you're here perhaps you can explain one thing. Why is it that seemingly half the undergraduate population is out to hound this woman into early retirement, if not an early grave? I don't understand it. I grant you she's not very attractive or especially scintillating company, but then neither are most of you students. Is that it? A cast of like attracting the hatred of like?"

"You're missing the point," I said angrily. "I'm not here to pursue Newcastle's bizarre vendetta. I like him about as much as you do. And I probably like Lafayette Jackson rather *more* than you do. I'm not here to create a scandal; I want to *avoid* one. Otherwise, this university will buy the goddamned things and then one day—I don't know when—someone's going to look real close at those papers and say, hey, wait a minute. And then you'll say to yourself, maybe that Yank was worth listening to."

"But just what am I to listen to? Why am I supposed to think any of what you've told me is true?"

I looked around the room for a moment before replying. Lidodes must have collected clocks; there were at least ten of them positioned on shelves among his books. Not one seemed to be ticking. "Before you dismiss what I've said, at least consider what I could possibly hope to gain by telling you all this. A libel suit? Getting sent down myself? A stay in the Warneford? What I've told you *is* true. So please, do me a favor and for God's sake make sure the papers Lafayette Jackson wants to sell get looked at very thoroughly. And not just by historians; find an ink man and a paper specialist. It won't take that long, or cost that much. If by some miracle the tests say the letters are authentic, then you'll simply look like a prudent and cautious man, and you can forget everything I've told you. You'll probably do that anyway."

"Probably," said Lidodes irritably, waving his hand to indicate the conversation was over.

Sixteen

🌺 *If love took* place in a vacuum, we could remove it with care, like clipping a single, perfect orchid blossom from a hot house plant, and study its power to change our lives. But instead it grows in a full bed of weeds; when we hold it up in memory we see ragwort and goldenrod, dandelions and rampion, crowding the single flower we have cultivated.

I started "seeing" Celia at an unpropitious time, for in less than two months I might well be returning to the States. Audrey made it clear she felt I was irresponsible and unfair to Celia; McCandles was openly noncommittal but, I think, agreed with his fiancée. A slight tension entered my relations with him, my closest Oxford friend, especially when my relationship with Celia grew intense. Only Bicker's high-spirited presence eased the strain.

There was little else to divert me during this period of waiting for my exam results. When term ended Lidodes promptly went to Greece for two weeks; Newcastle stayed in the Warneford; Lafayette Jackson could be seen in the Bodleian or ambling down the Broad, looking happy and unchanged. I had done my best and said my piece; there was nothing else I could or should do.

Then Bicker left for the States, sooner than expected, during a weekend when Celia and I had gone to the Cotswolds. He was not a man for formal farewells, or for formal anything. Yet like a lifeforce, undiluted, only slightly spurious, Bicker would crop up in my life again, I knew, move in and out of my future path like a train repeatedly crossing the sinuous trail of a river.

Still, I wished I had seen him off, and I said as much to McCandles when he came to see me that Sunday evening. Celia had left for London; I would join her there Wednesday.

"You know Bicker," said McCandles. "Friday night he decided he should go home, so Saturday he packed, and Sunday he upped and left. Anyway, he hadn't known you'd be away with Celia. None of us realized you were going to hit so heavily on some British girl six weeks before going home."

"Who says I'm going home?" I had mentioned my new wish to stay on at Oxford before, in fact had even told McCandles when I filled out my application to the English Faculty. But he had paid little attention. Now he was scornful. "Are you really *serious* about this?"

"Yes," I said simply.

"You'll need a First in your exams to be admitted. You don't honestly think you did that well. If you got a First you'll have made a laughingstock of the whole Oxford system. You haven't done *anything* for two years."

"I'm not going to get a First," I said, trying to conceal my growing irritation. I knew too well how little work I'd done. "A good Second Class degree will probably do the trick. That's not inconceivable, you know."

"What does Celia think about all this?"

"I suppose she's happy that I want to stay."

McCandles smiled sourly. "I figured that had something to do with it."

I didn't say anything. I cared a lot for Celia, but I knew that

I had decided to try to stay on in England before our relationship really began. "Well, Wilmarth," I said finally, "I guess we just have to agree to disagree. If you want to think I'm staying for Celia, fine. But I think you know that's not true."

"What am I supposed to think? You're just delaying things by staying on here. You don't want to become a professional student."

"If I did I wouldn't do it here. Better to live off the fat of an American graduate school, Christ knows."

"Why do it then?"

"Precisely because it isn't so pseudo-professional. Writing a thesis here doesn't condemn me to a life of trying to get tenure. It's the work that counts, not the career prospects. You feel about the treadmill exactly the way I do, admit it. It's just that you've resigned yourself to it a little earlier than I have. Don't worry; I'll be joining you, but not quite yet."

McCandles didn't press the point. I knew he was depressed about his own return to the States and to law school. He spoke for a few minutes about his forthcoming wedding in the autumn, trying, I felt, to cheer himself up. But then I explained that if my application were accepted at Oxford, the fact that his wedding would occur in the middle of term time meant there was a chance my new obligations as a post-graduate student would keep me from being there. He took this badly.

"Even Newcastle's coming," he complained.

"He is? When did he get out of the Warneford?"

"Yesterday."

"How is he? Is he going to be expelled?"

"Yes, yes," McCandles said impatiently. "He's due before the Proctors in three weeks time, just before Audrey and I fly back. Other than that, the boy's just the same, nuttier than a fruitcake. But forget Newcastle; why wouldn't you be able to fly back for the wedding?"

"We'll see."

"You could stay a while. We could play some golf."

"On your honeymoon?"

"Why not? It's not as if Audrey and I need time to get to know each other."

"Don't be an idiot," I said harshly, but regretted my tone when I saw the look of despair on McCandles' face. "Listen," I said, "I'll try to get back for the wedding. I can't promise."

I think we both knew I would be there in the end, but I was sufficiently irritated by his deprecating remarks about my plans to stay on that I wasn't going to volunteer anything just then. After a moment, McCandles finished his drink and, making his excuses, left. I felt badly that I wasn't sorry to see him go.

Ten days passed and I began to grow nervous about my results in exams. Then I found a note in my box telling me that I had a *viva,* a trial by ordeal imposed by the examiners on those students weak-minded enough to be caught straddling the borderline between one class and another. I had a bad five days before this oral exam, for it suddenly occurred to me that the *viva* might be between a low Second and a high Third, either of which would kill all chances of acceptance by the English Faculty. The *viva* didn't last very long; for although it turned out to be between a First and a Second, my ignorance of the Theory of Types was ruthlessly exposed. I was so relieved to learn I wasn't going to get a Third that it didn't seem to matter I wasn't going to get a First either.

Celia was on tour in the West Country but due back in London that night. I joined her and spent the next three days with her, leaving for Oxford on a Friday since Celia had a new tour beginning the next day. She had moved away from Earl's Court, to the ground-floor flat of a Georgian terrace house near Paddington. We slept in a big four-poster she'd been given by an aunt, but since we were still at the stage of not actually *sleeping* very much, I was tired when I returned to college that Friday afternoon. Fatigue was replaced by exhilaration when I found a letter in my box from the English Faculty, accepting me as a post-graduate student. I felt agitated and happy, so I left college and walked into Christ Church to tell McCandles.

I changed my mind before I reached his room. I had not seen him since our argument about my staying in England and he would hardly approve of my news. So I walked past his room, out into the lowering sun of Christ Church meadow, then along the Fellows Garden wall until I came to the Merton walk of cherry trees in the churchyard. The white blossoms were gone, for it was summer now, but I walked happily at the thought of seeing the next year's blossoms, too. There was no need to save the sight—one of my favorites—in my memory, for I would be seeing it again.

In Merton Street I debated which way to turn. Then, looking to my left, I saw Lafayette Jackson standing by the rear entrance to Christ Church. She wore a long khaki Burberry, the "Foreign Correspondent" kind—belted with epaulets—that tells you its wearer is American. From the way she looked around, either she was waiting for someone or was, improbably, lost. I walked over to her. "Mrs. Jackson?"

She looked at me, startled, and I had to reintroduce myself. Sometimes the anonymity of being a student is tedious. I didn't think it proper to offer my help; for all I knew she was making a carnal assignation. So I said only, "How are you?"

"Fine. Thank you. Well, actually, I'm trying to find my husband."

"Are you supposed to meet him here?"

"No, that's just it. I can't find the place where I am supposed to meet him. It's a pub called the Wheatsheaf." Her eyes moved around me as though this institution might materialize next to us at any moment.

"I know it." She must have missed the little alley. "I'm going that way myself. Let me show it to you."

"How kind," she said, almost mechanically, seeming very distracted as we walked up the slope of Oriel Square.

"So how have you been?" I said to make conversation as we walked.

"Busy. I have lots of packing to do."

"Really? Are you going back to the States?"

"Of course. Our visit's over now."

"Are you looking forward to getting back to Maryland? It must be awfully hot there this time of year."

She looked slowly at me for a brief moment, as if to see if I were pulling her leg. Deciding I wasn't, she relapsed into a look of detached preoccupation. "We're not going back to Maryland," she said shortly. "I've got a new appointment. In Hawaii."

"Hawaii? The University of Hawaii? I know some people there," I began, but she cut me off.

"No, not that university." Then, sensing I was waiting for an answer, she added, "It's a college actually, a brand-new college. I'm going out to run their History department."

"Congratulations," I said insincerely, as we turned up the alley towards the pub. I knew something must have happened, but what?

Howard was standing outside, wearing a raincoat like his wife's. As we approached him, he drained the glass in his hand and set it down on an exterior window sill. He came forward to greet us, and Lafayette explained my role in her arrival. He seemed dimly to remember me. I felt unready to leave with so much unexplained, but Howard made no move to keep me with them, and why should he have? I struggled to think of something which would prolong the conversation and allow me to discover what had happened to change their plans. And what about the papers?

"Well," I said, trying to think quickly, "it's been very nice meeting you both again." I turn expressly to Howard. "I understand you're moving to Hawaii. Good luck out there. But I'm sure I'll be seeing you two here again." They nodded abstractedly and I added, "Next summer. Right?"

"What?" said Howard, puzzled.

"I mean, the papers, the island papers your wife is selling here, and the new library. I just assumed you'd be back on, uh, related business."

It was Howard's turn to stare at me suspiciously, to search for mockery in my eyes. Lafayette suddenly seemed embarrassed. "We won't be back," she said sadly. "The papers, they're going to Hawaii, too. Other colleges have libraries, you know," she added, and for the first time I detected a hint of, what? irony? possibly the beginnings of bitterness? in her soft Southern voice.

"Really?" I said, perhaps a little rudely, but I was astonished. Somehow, then, word had got out about the island letters. And now she must know, too, that they were phony, perhaps even that her husband had connived in their fabrication. No wonder she seemed depressed.

"Yep," said Howard, looking at his watch. "Young man," he said, sounding more like a reputable banker than the two-bit crook I now took him for, "you have to go where the money is. Oxford and Harvard and Yale, I tell you, they're fine enough—a little hoity-toity maybe—but fine I'm sure. But when you're talking about the bottom line in the balance sheet, you don't care about its breeding. Young fellow, *you can't eat prestige.*"

Lafayette looked ready to crawl under the pavement; for a brief moment I thought she was going to burst into tears. I felt a deep resentment at her husband for the pain he was causing her. So I said with mock-innocence, "I got it, Mr. Jackson." He looked at me eagerly. "You've gone and found yourself a back-up buyer."

And saying goodbye I walked quickly up the alley towards the High as Howard asked Lafayette angrily, "Who the hell was that?"

I walked quickly back to college, determined to find Krattenstein. I felt like a second-rate detective, without a clear brief, not even sure who his client was, making the same old mistake of becoming more interested in the case than in his retainer.

Krattenstein lived high above Chapel Quad in an alcove set of two rooms that I'd never visited, despite our frequent conversations. They turned out to be somber, formal, much like Krattenstein himself, who was wearing a tie under his jersey when he answered the door. The walls of his room were covered by beautiful oak book shelves; I realized Krattenstein lived in a former Fellow's suite.

"Come on in," he said politely, and I walked into his sitting room and stared at his books. Above his desk were several series of large history volumes. Thinking of my own eclectic collection—poetry, novels, many modern books with bright, arresting dust jackets—I thought, here are a real scholar's tools. There was even a six-volume history of Canada, although I forebore saying how amazed I was that Canada actually *had* six volumes of history.

Krattenstein sat down again at his desk and motioned me to the comfortable armchair by his electric wall fire. "I'd offer you a coffee, but I've run out. And," he said, pointing to his open notebook, "I haven't had time to get any more."

Knowing Krattenstein, this didn't strike me as unlikely. He worked hard, but rarely allowed his academic concerns to cloud his common sense; his occasional confusions were real. "I don't need a coffee, anyway."

He nodded and looked at his hands. He was too polite to ask what then I did need. "I've just seen Lafayette Jackson," I said. "And Howard."

Krattenstein smiled fleetingly and looked again at his hands. "Newcastle must be pleased with the way things have turned out for her."

"You tell me. I've been away. I know he's out of the Warneford but that's about all I do know. Now Lafayette tells me she's going to teach at some Hawaiian college no one's heard of and Howard says the papers from that Mississippi island are going there as well. What happened?"

"Perhaps unwisely from his point of view, Howard Jackson deposited a large proportion of the letters he and Lafayette wanted to sell to the university with Lidodes, doubtless thinking he'd simply sit on them—you know how much interest Lidodes has in American history. Probably much to Howard's surprise, Lidodes had them carefully examined by experts; who said the letters couldn't have been written before D-Day. Since they are supposed to document Southern life in the 1840's, the disparity could not be explained away."

"I'll say. What was it? The paper? Was the paper wrong?"

Krattenstein smiled wryly. "The paper, as I understand it, was made in Italy, probably after 1951. The ink is of a vulgar American make, almost certainly less than thirty years old. The handwriting was especially interesting. It seems at least two different hands were employed writing the letters said to come from one man. Frankly, you name something that could be bogus and it's probably in those letters somewhere."

"What did Lidodes do?"

"He told the committee for the library. They're the ones who have to approve the purchase. Naturally, with such evidence in hand, they've decided not to buy the papers."

"And the Jacksons know. I mean they know that the world knows?"

"Yes. Lidodes had the unenviable task of telling them. In fact, I think he told Howard Jackson, not Lafayette. Chicanery seems more in his line than hers. I'm not even sure Lafayette would have known."

"No. I'm absolutely sure she didn't. I bet she was devastated. God," I said guiltily, thinking of my role in this exposure. I was very surprised that Lidodes had acted.

"I wouldn't feel bad about it, James. It would have come out in the end anyway."

"It might not have."

"Okay, possibly not. But it should have. Scholarship becomes fairly pointless when you're working with forged materials."

"How did you know I was involved in this? Did Lidodes tell you?"

"Yes. Don't look so irritated, James. You can hardly blame him. He wanted to know whether I thought you were trustworthy. This was just before he went to Greece. He must have commissioned the analysis of the letters then, because as soon as he was back he confronted Howard Jackson. Since then he's had occasion to mention your name more than once. Not ungratefully, I might add."

"So the Jacksons now flee in disgrace to Hawaii."

Krattenstein nodded. "And none too soon. Word may have already reached the University of Maryland. Dons are as discreet as the next group of people, maybe even more so, but it would be unnatural to expect this to stay totally secret within the profession. This new college in Hawaii won't know yet and Lafayette will be virtually impossible to dislodge when it does find out. She has a large reputation after all; it will take a long time to lose it."

"It's awfully tainted after this, even for the University of

Pineapple, or wherever she's going. Most historians don't rely on jimmied evidence, not that she knew it was."

"No, thank God they don't. But if things ever got truly nasty—I mean, accusations of fraud by her colleagues or the Modern History Association—she can, rightly you say, claim ignorance and blame it all on the bookseller who supplied the letters in the first place."

"Smiley. Or on Howard, for that matter."

"Yes, from what Lidodes told me he's the villain of the piece. Isn't he?"

"I'll say."

"It's a blow to Lafayette, of course, but there has been no *public* scandal. She can continue to make a living."

"Not at any reputable institution."

"No, you're right. But certainly at what you call the University of Pineapple she'll be all right."

We sat thinking for a moment. Then Krattenstein opened his desk drawer and greatly to my surprise took out a pint bottle of rye whiskey. He ignored my wide and rather eager eyes, got two mugs from his bathroom, and poured us each a great slug of the stuff.

"To the University of Pineapple," he said, lifting his mug. "And to your recent success in exams."

"Relative success," I said, also drinking. "But thank you. Tell me, what about the Robert E. Lee papers? The ones in Rhodes House. Are they phony, too?"

Krattenstein paused for a second and looked thoughtful. "Who knows? I don't believe any checks were made on them."

"Besides Newcastle's." And I told him of the findings of Hunnicot & Sons.

"So that's what he was doing breaking into Rhodes House. I figured it was something like that. But in any case you've just said they passed his test. So there isn't any reason for Lidodes or anyone else to doubt them."

"Of course there is. They come from the same source as the island letters. I'd bet anything they're no good, either." Krattenstein said nothing, so I continued. "The difference is that, unlike Lafayette's papers, the Lee letters are already part of the university's collections. They've already been bought. If doubts are thrown on their authenticity, then there would be a public scandal. There would be no sweeping that under the rug."

"I suppose not," he conceded.

"Of course not," I said sharply, then added almost admiringly, "Lidodes isn't stupid. The ironic thing is that he'd never have caught out the papers of Lafayette Jackson if Newcastle hadn't first tried to raise the alarm."

"Don't try telling Lidodes that. He virtually has a complex about Newcastle. He might give you credit for coming to him about Howard Jackson's chicanery but don't expect a soft spot in his heart for Newcastle."

This was depressing news. "Without Newcastle none of this would have emerged."

"Why not? You still would have heard Howard Jackson talking about it."

"I wouldn't have had a clue what he was talking about. In fact, if Newcastle's nutty obsession hadn't attracted my friend McCandles' fancy, I wouldn't know what a Jackson was, much less some antebellum Mississippi correspondence. The one person Lidodes still hates—assuming you're right and he no longer finds me utterly contemptible—is the one who helped him the most."

"You're awfully fond of situational irony."

"Maybe so," I said slowly, swallowing the rest of the whiskey. "But this is one irony you should point out to your friend Lidodes. You know I'm right. It could even be argued that Newcastle himself saved the university from a catastrophe. But what's his reward? Expulsion. Shattering his career hopes. Even Lafayette, sitting out at Pineapple U., knowing the husband she loves is a complete crook, and that her famous book is based on a pack of lies—even she looks positively golden compared to that poor bastard. And he didn't even do anything wrong. Someone really ought to point that out to Lidodes. You could tell him that even Machiavelli once said that craftiness should always be tempered by fairness."

"Where did he say that? In *The Prince*?"

"Of course not. But Lidodes won't know that. He probably thinks Machiavelli's the headwaiter's name at the *Luna Caprese*. Thanks for the whiskey."

Seventeen

July *was theatening* to end and I began my new work with enthusiasm. All thesis titles sound ridiculous, and mine was no exception: I had been admitted to write one with the provisional title of "Returning Home: The Expatriate Experiences of Henry James, T. S. Eliot and Ernest Hemingway." Nothing seemed to link their individual decisions to live abroad, but I enjoyed my reading and it was a great relief to read things I was naturally drawn to. I also liked my appointed adviser, an eminent English Literature don who came from Milwaukee. He had a young Italian wife with dark doe eyes who welcomed the chance to talk with someone who had heard of Oriana Fallaci. They seemed happy to have me over for a drink, which was large and American-style, served in the garden of their Norham Road house, and they told me to bring Celia the next time.

She came to Oxford for the last weekend of July. Despite the attractions of having Emily as my scout, I had decided not to live the next year in college. We spent the weekend accordingly in the countryside outside Oxford, looking for a place for me to live. Saturday proved hopeless—there was nothing available but brick cow sheds or eight-room cottages I couldn't afford. But on Sunday, purely by chance, going down a private driveway in desperation, we came to a large Edwardian house with two small adjoining cottages. Encountering the slightly batty lady of the house clipping the hedge on her drive, we spoke to her in slightly offhand tones for ten minutes, then accepted her offer of one of the cottages as of September 1.

I came back to college that evening with Celia, happy about the prospects for my new life. We had dinner at the pub across the street then returned to my room. Celia read back issues of the *Spectator* until she was bored to tears while I tackled Hemingway's early journalism manfully. At ten o'clock I poured us each a large drink.

"You know Wilmarth and Audrey are leaving for the States tomorrow?"

"Yes," I said as I handed her a glass. "He left me a note on Friday. They're leaving first thing in the morning."

"We ought to get up and see them off."

I didn't say anything. McCandles' note had been curt (as if informing Hubert of his departure), and our recent relations sufficiently strained that I'd almost decided not to go and say goodbye.

"Don't you think?" added Celia.

"I don't know. I'm not sure he'd care if I did."

"Don't be like him. There's nothing tough about that, you know. You can put the Hemingway down. Once I read how he left his first wife I realized he wasn't such a brave man after all."

I threw the book on my bed. "What am I supposed to say to that? I've got through my exams, found a place to live, been accepted by the English Faculty; I'm all set now. So why spoil it by talking to McCandles? He doesn't approve of what I'm doing; he made that clear enough. I thought he was my friend."

"He is your friend."

"That's what you say. To tell you the truth, he doesn't even approve of us. Neither does Audrey for that matter."

"I don't need you to tell me that. But it doesn't matter. They're your friends; they're our friends. Whether they approve or not."

"How can you say that?"

"Why not? Do all your friends have to think just like you do? That's a lot to ask from a friend."

"That's not fair. Wilmarth hasn't been aboveboard. He's got worries of his own, so he takes them out on me."

"Fine. Maybe that's what you can do to help him right now. Stop talking about what's fair; no one's counting, you know. If you don't say goodbye it's no skin off your back. For the time being your life's here; you're not making any changes. But think about Wilmarth. He's leaving, and going back to God knows what. You think he's being entirely conventional, but I bet you he's scared to death. He doesn't have any idea if he'll be doing something he enjoys, or is any good at, or gives two figs for. You don't have that problem. You may half-starve doing what you want but I know you'll do it. You're like that, and Wilmarth's not. So don't act the wounded, sensitive chap. Be a good friend and go see him off."

"That's some speech," I said half-sarcastically.

She drained her glass and held it out for more. "Not bad, if I say so myself. And true, every single word of it. Don't confuse effective rhetoric with lying, you academic Yank."

The day began in hazy mist when my alarm went off at seven-thirty. By the time I smuggled Celia out of my room past Emily's prying eyes the sky was clearing, and soon cloudless. There was no time for breakfast and we hurried across St. Aldates to Christ Church. Under Tom Tower stood two black London-style taxis. Their drivers were beginning to load the luggage stacked by the porter's gate. Audrey stood by the college entrance, supervising the loading procedure, and I realized that both taxis were for McCandles' accumulated gear. He was nowhere in sight.

"Do you need some help, Audrey?" I asked.

"Not now," she said. "We could have used you ten minutes ago. I think we may have sent one of the porters to an early death with that." She pointed to an enormous sea trunk that stood amidst a pile of boxes and suitcases, framed pictures and rolled-up posters, a small rug and a vast brass spittoon. "I'd let the drivers do the loading if I were you," said Audrey. "Otherwise there may not be enough room. I told Wilmarth we should have had a third taxi."

"Are you excited?" Celia asked her kindly.

Audrey nodded vigorously and I suddenly understood that she didn't really like England. Not surprising: her social snobbery went unsatisfied in London, where nobody gave a hoot about when her forebears reached the Plymouth shore. To be charitable, she had undoubtedly had a miserable time, waiting tables while her fiancé enjoyed the 20th century equivalent of a Gentleman's Tour. But now her moment was coming, I could see her thinking, and she was just a plane ride away from the restitution of her self-importance.

"Miss," one of the cabdrivers said to her, "we seem to have got it all in. We're ready anytime you are."

"Thank you." She turned and looked through the arch of Tom Quad. "Where is he? If we miss this flight I swear I'll make him take me First Class on the next one out."

Celia winked at me and I restrained a laugh. "Relax Audrey," I told her. "I'll go find the fellah, just you wait here."

"Don't bother," said Celia, for McCandles had appeared, strolling past the figure of Mercury in the middle of the quad. He wore a straw hat, slanted jauntily to one side, a white short-sleeved shirt, khaki trousers, and blood-colored penny loafers with no socks. In one arm he cradled a picture, in the other he swung a bottle of gin by its neck. He was whistling and as he drew near he recognized us and his face broke into a broad smile.

"I wasn't sure you'd be here," he called out as he drew near.

"Why not? If we can survive a lunatic like Andrew Mercy then we'll always be friends."

He laughed and came up to us. "Hello, my dear," he said to Celia. "Has my wife-to-be persuaded you of the virtues of marriage?"

"Wilmarth," said Audrey warningly.

"It's early days, Wilmarth," I said, putting an arm around Celia. "I have to get her into bed first."

Celia groaned and McCandles laughed again. "You know," he declared, lifting his arms and their booty, "I almost forgot these two. I'm not sure which would prove the greater loss. And then I saw you standing here and I realized one of them should stay behind with you. I was going to let you choose which one, but I've always tried to save you from yourself and I can't stop trying now." He put down the bottle of gin on the stone floor. "You can buy your own gin anytime, but perhaps when you two are sitting around like a pair of old soaks, you'll think of me if you have this to look at." And he handed me the picture, which was the Rowlandson watercolor of the drunken fox-hunters.

I didn't say anything for a minute, just looked fondly at my departing friend. "I've got to thank Andrew Mercy after all, or we'd have never met," I said finally.

McCandles looked at his watch. "We had better go, Audrey, before tears as big as horse turds start running down young James' cheeks." He suddenly looked around. "I thought Mr. Mercy's successor might be here to see me off."

"Who?" asked Audrey, dreading another farewell.

"Young Newcastle," McCandles announced. He walked

towards the taxis. Audrey got in after pecking me quickly on the cheek. Celia stood by the cab window to say goodbye to her.

"Have you seen him?" McCandles asked me.

I shook my head. "Not since he got sent down."

"He didn't get sent down. I should have told you, but we have not been precisely in close communion lately. Newcastle got off with a reprimand. He was officially reproved for excessive zeal, but they didn't send him down."

"You must be kidding."

"No. That pompous don in your college must have taken pity on him."

"Lidodes."

"That's the man. Newcastle can now stay on and do a thesis."

"I shouldn't think Hubert will be very pleased."

"Oh, he's not doing it with Hubert anymore. He's switched fields."

"Wait," I said holding up a hand. "Don't tell me. He's switched to British history."

"That's right. How did you know?"

"I didn't; I can smell it. And he's switched to an earlier period, right? Something in the 15th century probably, something to do with the Wars of the Roses."

"Exactly. And he wants—"

I interrupted. "He wants Lidodes to be his supervisor."

McCandles laughed heartily. "You certainly know your Newcastle." He took a final look around. "I guess he's not going to show up. That's gratitude for you," and we both laughed. "After all we've done for the boy. He'll never have such an interested audience again. What a story it will make for New Haven. I bet even Yale can't match him."

"I can guarantee that."

"What a pity. Well, he's your responsibility now."

"What?"

"Sure, now that I'm leaving. You know what I mean."

"Actually, Wilmarth, he's been my responsibility for a while."

"Good old serious James," said McCandles. "You should know by now it never mattered all that much." He stuck out his hand and we shook. "In any case, take good care of yourself. When this place gets to *you*, catch the first plane and come home."

"You'll see me before then anyway," I said, and when McCandles raised his eyebrows I added with a jerk of my head in Audrey's direction, "when you lose your freedom this autumn."

"You'll still be Best Man then?"

"Of course," I said. "I wouldn't miss it for all the tea in China."

"You mean the Mercy in Macon."

"No, I mean—"

"Come on you guys," Audrey said impatiently, "the drivers are waiting."

"So long, Wilmarth," I said, and he kissed Celia goodbye, shook my hand, and got into the cab. The taxi performed a smart U-turn, followed by the second bag-laden cab, and the small convoy moved away up the street.

I stood with Celia watching the taxis drive off. As they turned at Carfax the straw boater appeared out of one window, waved vigorously in the air. "I'll miss him," I said sadly.

"Of course you will," said Celia, or words to that effect, for her sentence was obscured by someone shouting across the street. I looked up and there was Newcastle, struggling up St. Aldates on a black bicycle, shouting McCandles' name. "Goodbye Wilmarth," he cried, but he was too late, for the taxis had already turned the Carfax corner and sped out of sight. Newcastle suddenly braked on the street, in front of

St. Aldates Church. An Audi swerved to avoid him, and an elderly lady on a bicycle almost ran into his standing figure. "Careful," she said sternly.

"Thatcherite!" Newcastle shouted back at her as she pedalled slowly away. He looked mournfully up the street.

"You've missed him, I'm afraid," I yelled across the street. But he didn't hear me, and after a moment he turned his bike around and wheeled it down the side street towards my college. He was going to see his new putative adviser.

I took a deep breath and looked up at the squat bulk of Wren's Tower. Poor Lidodes: how he would come to regret his admirable act of leniency. It might take one term, it might take two, but the day would come when his inadequacies would be fished out with infinite pains by his new student and held up, in journals and reviews across the world, for all the members of his profession to behold. If Lidodes had ever fallen, ever indulged in the smallest lie, the most insignificant fabrication, I could now be sure that Newcastle would unearth it.

"Who was that?" asked Celia.

I took her by the arm and led her down St. Aldates. "No one of any importance at all," I told her. "Someone from my past. Now let me show you the prettiest walk in Oxford."

The Tormenting
of Lafayette Jackson

was set on the Linotron 202 in Bembo, a design based on
the types used by Venetian scholar–publisher Aldus Manutius
in the printing of *De Aetna*, written by Pietro Bembo and
published in 1495. The original characters were cut in 1490
by Francesco Griffo who, at Aldus's request, later cut the
first italic types. Originally adapted by the English Monotype
Company, Bembo is now widely available and highly re-
garded. It remains one of the most elegant, readable, and
widely used of all book faces.

Composed by Chappel Typesetting, Athens, Ohio. Printed
and bound by Haddon Craftsmen, Scranton, Pennsylvania.
Designed by Virginia Evans.